PILGRENNON'S BEACON

MANDA BENSON

-Book one of Pilgrennon's Children-

TANGENTRINE

www.tangentrine.com

www.tangentrine.com

Second edition published by Tangentrine 2024
First edition published by Tangentrine 2010

Typeset in InDesign

ISBN: 978-1-917231-01-5

*"Relativity applies to physics,
not ethics."*

-ALBERT EINSTEIN

*With thanks to:
D.J. Cockburn, Stacey Buckby, Arthur
Dorrance, Jo & Sammy, and Nerine Dorman,
and with special thanks to J.D. Williams.*

–1–

DANA jabbed the button on the pelican crossing, but the word WAIT remained illuminated. She threw a glance to the street behind her and looked up at the green light facing the road. She concentrated on that light and told it to change.

The green light went off, the red one came on, and the green walking figure above the button lit up. Cars slowed as they rolled towards the crossing. Dana didn't wait to be sure they'd stopped before she ran across the road.

As soon as she reached the pavement on the opposite side she told the light to change back. Engines revved behind her. Over her shoulder she saw Abigail and her two henchgirls reach the far side too late, a river of rush-hour traffic separating them from her. Abigail met Dana's backward glance with a murderous glare.

Dana hurried on, the straps of her school bag jarring her shoulders with every step. Slimy autumn leaves covered the path, making it treacherous for running. If Dana concentrated, she could imagine a map showing her all the roads and streets and their names. An alley not far ahead offered a different route to Pauline and Graeme's house. Perhaps if she went that way, Abigail would lose track of her and give up.

She ran faster, holding her breath against the stink of dogs' business lining the alley. She turned at the end and set off down another street. A group of boys wandered along the opposite pavement. "Dictionary girl!" they jeered. Dana ignored them, reaching the end of the street and turning on to the road where Pauline and Graeme lived. The house was up ahead, only a few more yards, but she could see neither Pauline's nor Graeme's cars parked nearby.

She jumped the gate at the end of the drive and ran to the front door, pushing the bell and hammering on the uPVC. "Duncan!" she shouted, breath coming in ragged gasps. "Let me in!"

Duncan was probably listening to MP3s. He might not be able to hear her. Dana went to the front window and banged on the double glazing. "Cale!" Dana could just make out her brother's shape in the shadows beyond her own reflection, on the sofa with his legs curled beneath him. *Cale, open the door*, she thought. Cale curled up and pulled a cushion over his head, ignoring her.

The door opened, and there stood Duncan, greasy dark-brown hair overhanging his acne-cratered face. The thunder of drums and the wailing of electric guitars issued faintly from the plugs in his ears. Dana squeezed past him, flinging her bag down in the hall on her way through to the dining room, and sat at the table without taking off her coat.

After a moment, she heard the front door close. She sensed Duncan coming closer from the signal his mobile phone gave off. When she glanced up, he was standing in the doorway, looking awkward. Duncan had the same sturdy build as Pauline, and Graeme's height. It was easy to see why bullies didn't pick on him.

"Wanna sandwich?" he said.

Dana sniffed and nodded.

She put her hands over her face, listening to Duncan clattering about in the kitchen and the signal from his mobile phone, and another signal from a computer upstairs that had been left on. Her throat became tight, her nose blocked itself up, and an aching, burning sensation spread from her eyes across her face. Day after day. Why wouldn't Abigail Swift just leave her alone?

The microwave beeped. Duncan returned and set a plate down by her elbow.

Dana sniffed hard, gulping and wiping her eyes. "Thanks."

"It's all right," said Duncan quietly, and went away.

Dana took a bite of sandwich and chewed, trying to drown out the horrible feelings in her face. Duncan only seemed able to make one kind of food: two slices of bread with cheese and brown sauce in the middle, warmed up in a microwave.

The front door opened. Pauline's voice: "Dana?" Pauline came to stand in the dining-room doorway. "Dana, why did you go off on your own? I was waiting for you outside the school! I went in and your teacher didn't know where you were. We looked all over for you!"

Graeme appeared behind Pauline, still wearing his work suit. "What's going on?" he said.

Dana stared at the sandwich in front of her. "It was Abigail, again."

Pauline and Graeme exchanged glances.

"All right, Dana." Graeme's voice sounded tired. "Have you got homework to do?"

"Yes."

"Then you'd better go upstairs and do it before we make dinner. I know you're not feeling well now, but it has to be done."

Dana paused outside the living room on the way to the stairs. "Hi, Cale," she said, but her brother's eyes were shut and he didn't respond.

Often adults would say Cale closed his eyes because he was overwhelmed, but Dana knew he was thinking and he didn't want the pictures from his eyes to get in the way of the images in his mind. Dana could always tell what Cale was thinking, but never anyone else. Right now he was thinking about beetles. Cale had found out about beetles soon after they had both come to live with Pauline and Graeme and Duncan, when they had all gone to a museum in London together. Dana had liked the dinosaur bones, but Cale had spent the whole time fascinated with dead beetles inside glass cases in shabby wooden drawers. When Graeme said it was time to go, the locks on all the museum doors had jammed. Cale refused to go, even when the museum staff said they had to leave because it was closing time. Graeme and Pauline had ended up dragging him by the arms through the fire exit.

Cale's eyelids quivered. He pushed Dana out of his mind without a movement. Dana wished she could shut the world out like that when things overwhelmed her.

In her bedroom, Dana opened her homework on the desk. Graeme had sent her upstairs so he could talk to Pauline about her, she supposed, but the stereo downstairs had been left on and she could hear their voices clearly through the microphone on it. "I don't see why Dana should be marginalised," he was saying. "It's the other girl who's got a problem!"

"I'm going to speak to that headmaster tomorrow," Pauline said. "While I was looking for Dana at the school, I got talking to that bloody teacher, and do you know what she said?" Pauline's voice had risen to an indignant pitch. "She *insinuated* Dana isn't *properly* autistic, that she puts it on to *get attention!*"

Dana put her hand in her skirt pocket and took out the 13-amp fuse Graeme had given her from a toaster that had broken a few weeks ago. The fuse had brown writing on it and fitted comfortably into her hand. She held it tightly.

After dinner, which was toad-in-the-hole and boiled cabbage, Dana went back to her bedroom to finish off her homework.

A knock sounded through the panelled wood of the door.

"Who is it?"

The door slowly opened a few inches to reveal Duncan's eye, the bottom of his face concealed behind a DVD disc he was holding up. "Wanna play?"

In his bedroom, Duncan put the DVD labelled *Pillage and Burn* into the drawer on his computer. Dana took her seat on a cushion, her game controller in her hands. Duncan had set a bowl filled with prawn-flavour shell-shaped crisps between their cushions.

Both looked over their shoulders at the sound of the door opening, but it was only Cale, who slunk in with a bowl and spoon in his hands, and sat on Duncan's bed under the heavy metal posters covering the wall. Cale didn't like the prawn crisps, didn't like their crunchiness or the salty-sweet vinegar taste. What Cale liked best was what Graeme called frogspawn: a bowl of warm tapioca made with plain full-cream milk without any sugar or flavouring added. He liked the bland taste and the feel of the soft, squishy globes on his tongue.

The game loaded. Dana and Duncan selected their characters. When Duncan had first played the game, he'd had to choose from a human, a giant, a dwarf, or an elf. He had at first tried to make a giant, an enormous man with bulging, stringy muscles, wearing a pair of green briefs. Duncan hadn't liked him much, and had changed the sex symbol on the character creation screen to female and made a giantess in a bikini instead. The camera in the game followed the character around from behind, and Duncan said if he had to look at someone's bum, he'd rather it be a woman's bum than a man's.

In this game, it was possible for two people to play together, so after Duncan had played it by himself for a few days, he'd let Dana make a character to play with him. Dana had made a dwarf with long golden hair and a beard. The female symbol on the character creation screen had been greyed out for dwarfs, so Dana had said she thought this dwarf was a girl dwarf, because a few weeks before, Duncan had showed her the *Lord of the Rings* films from his DVD collection, and Dana remembered Gimli the dwarf said dwarf women had beards and that other people couldn't tell them apart from dwarf men, which Duncan had thought was funny and said was probably right.

Duncan had tried to get Cale to make a character once, but he didn't want to, even though he did like to watch when Duncan and Dana played.

The game loaded the place they had last visited. Duncan's giantess and Dana's dwarf stood outside the castle of an evil sorcerer. They set off across the drawbridge, the giantess beating down leering orcs with her axe and shield, the dwarf casting magic spells to smite down the enemies and heal the warrior. Duncan, preoccupied with the action, stared intently at the screen, not noticing that although the control was in Dana's hands, she never pressed any of the buttons. He'd explained to her when he'd first shown her the game, *this is how you steer the character, this button does that*. But Dana found she had only to think what she wanted the character to do. She could also cheat: make the enemies die faster, or the giantess's health stay high when she would have died. But it was too easy that way, and neither of them enjoyed it so much. So Dana contented herself with the occasional dodge of a critical hit, and played within the rules.

If she concentrated hard, she could even see the game as though she were the dwarf herself, running around the game world under its gradient sky-screen, among buildings and terrains and blocky tree forms pasted with pixellated textures.

Around the castle they ran, killing baddies and looting treasure, until they found the long winding staircase to the highest tower, and up, up they went, for the confrontation with the evil wizard. He cast dark magic spells against them like smouldering skulls, but with Duncan's fighting and Dana's healing, they defeated him, and his gold and robe and book of magic fell to the floor for them to loot.

"Look here." Dana noticed an anomaly in the code. "I think there's a hidden door behind the tapestry in the wall behind the wizard."

Duncan opened the door and the screen faded out.

Duncan shifted forward on his cushion. "This must be an Easter Egg level!"

When the screen faded back in, the giantess and the dwarf had rematerialised in a dingy dungeon. Corpses in various states of decomposition and with assorted body parts missing were strewn about the room, lying on the floor, hanging by the wrists from manacles, or slumped inside iron maidens.

The instant Dana's and Duncan's characters materialised, the corpses suddenly came to life. Broken zombies crept across the floor, groaning and reaching grotesquely, and headless bodies staggered towards them with arms outstretched.

The giantess assumed the *en garde* position; the dwarf began casting a spell.

Then Pauline's voice interrupted. "For goodness' sake, Duncan, it's nearly ten o'clock! Turn this thing off! What is this rubbish, anyway? It looks too scary for Dana."

"It's not!" Dana protested. They'd both looked away from the screen, and now the giantess and the dwarf were lying on the floor, killed by the undead, beneath words that read *Game Over*.

-2-

"**C**AN I stay at home today?"

Graeme was kneeling on the carpet, taking apart the plug on Pauline's hairdryer. "Pauline and I have to go to work, Dana. And Duncan has to go to school, too. There'll be nobody here. You'd be bored."

"No, I wouldn't," said Dana.

Graeme put down the screwdriver and carefully turned the plug over. It came in two, like a walnut, and inside it the black cable split into three coloured wires attached to the prongs.

"This brown one is the live wire." Graeme showed her. "And there's the fuse." He prised out the little cylinder with his screwdriver.

"Come on, Graeme, there's not time to tell Dana how it works," Pauline said. "Just put the other fuse in so I can dry my hair."

"Here, hold the broken fuse for me, please, Dana."

The fuse had orange writing on it. Three amps. Graeme pressed a replacement fuse into the plug.

"Cale, will you stop playing with that keyboard and get ready!" Pauline called. Cale did not answer. The ponderous stream of notes coming from his bedroom continued. "Duncan, what do you want to have for dinner on Thursday?"

"Mum, I've told you I want motorbike lessons!" Duncan's voice came from behind the closed door of his bedroom.

"We've told you, you're not having a bike. You can wait until you're seventeen and have driving lessons!"

An object thumped against the wall of Duncan's room.

Graeme put the plug back together and finished tightening the screw. He plugged it back into the wall and switched it on. The motor on the hairdryer started.

"I'll have to go now, or I'll be late." Graeme hugged Dana, his coarse, greying sideburn scratching her cheek. "Listen to what the teacher says at school and try to learn." He stood up and shouted, "Cale, you listen to what the teacher says as well. Bye, Duncan!" He turned and kissed Pauline, who was hurriedly drying her hair, and went downstairs, grabbing his jacket from the banister.

Pauline brought Dana in early for school. Instead of waiting in the noisy chaos of the yard as usual before lessons started, Dana was directed into the empty classroom, where she sat at her desk while Pauline and Miss Robinson talked in the corridor. Dana couldn't hear what they were saying, only see their mouths moving through the glass in the door.

She fumbled with the fuses in her skirt pocket, her attention drawn by the white box with the blinking lights on the wall in the far corner of the classroom. She'd asked what it was the first day she'd come to the school, and Miss Robinson had told her it was called a wireless LAN and it told the computers what to do. Dana could get it to tell her things too, like the news and answers to questions.

She started at the noise of the door opening. Pauline had gone, and Miss Robinson came in accompanied by a girl with shoulder-length blonde hair and a lilac hairband.

"Dana, I want you and Laura to stick together today and help each other out," said Miss Robinson as Laura took her seat beside Dana's. Laura had been introduced to Dana when she'd started at the school, as a 'buddy' to help her find her way around, but Dana never knew what to say to her. Laura wasn't unpleasant, but she only ever wanted to talk about singers in pop bands, and Dana didn't know or care much about that sort of thing.

The bell rang, and children clamoured in the corridor outside and poured into the classroom. Miss Robinson stood beside her desk with her arms folded, her fuchsia-painted lips drawn into a thin line, until they were all sitting in their places and being quiet.

Miss Robinson began. "Who here can tell me what a comma is?"

The light flickered on the wLAN box in the corner. Dana said, "Comma, noun, the punctuation mark, indicating a slight pause and used when there is a listing of items or to separate a non-restrictive cause from a main clause."

The other children roared with laughter. Dana could feel her face going red. Miss Robinson raised her hand for silence and said, "Dana, we've discussed this before. If you think you know the answer, you need to raise your hand and wait until you're asked to speak. If we don't all obey the rules, it's not fair and other people don't get a turn."

Dana put up her hand. She looked about, but no-one else's hand was up.

"All right, Dana," said Miss Robinson.

Dana repeated the answer. A few of the children sniggered.

"That's good, but can you think of another way of putting it, that'll be a bit easier to understand, Dana?"

Dana looked back at Miss Robinson, an anxious knot in her chest.

"Can anyone else think of one?" said Miss Robinson.

After a moment, a boy near the back raised his hand. "Julian?"

"Is it like when you make a list, and you put them between the things on the list?"

"Yes, good! So when you make a list, you put commas between the words on the list." Miss Robinson began to type, and words appeared on the wall screen behind her. "So, if we're going shopping, can anyone think of something we'd have on our list?"

Beside Dana, Laura put up her hand. "Chips, Miss."

Miss Robinson nodded. "Chips." *Chips*, appeared on the screen.

"Burgers, Miss," offered a boy. The list became *Chips, burgers,*

"Abigail?"

"Condoms, Miss," said Abigail in a sullen voice. The other children laughed.

Miss Robinson rolled her eyes, but added *condoms*, to the list. "Quiet now, please. At least Abigail is thinking responsibly, although I hope you'll have to try harder than just chips and burgers to impress. All right, I think you all have the idea." Miss Robinson finished off the list with *salad*. "Now, for the next exercise, I'd like you form an orderly line and each collect a computer."

The children all scraped back their chairs and formed a queue along the back of the classroom to pick up a laptop. As Dana carried her computer back to the table, Abigail twisted in her seat. Her foot hit Dana in the ankles. The computer slipped from her hands as Dana lost her balance, grabbing a chair and overturning it as she fell. It hit the ground with a crash, the screen breaking off the keyboard by its hinges. The computer's tiny heartbeat disappeared from the back of Dana's mind. At the same time, something on the carpet stabbed her forearm — a stray drawing pin.

The smell of sweaty feet and the feel of the rough carpet were overwhelming. Miss Robinson loomed above, featureless in the glare from the fluorescent tubes on the ceiling. Heat flooded Dana's face and a hot prickly sensation crawled up her back. The light on the wLAN box blinked rapidly.

Abigail said, "She tripped over her own feet, Miss."

"Oh, dear," said Miss Robinson. "Dana, this computer's broken."

Anger boiled over. Dana hated Abigail with all the hate she had in her. She wished Abigail would get a horrible painful disease and die from it, and she wished Abigail's parents would die too. The light on the wLAN blinked faster.

"It wasn't my fault!"

The lights went out with a loud bang. The feeling of the wLAN disappeared. Dana couldn't tell which direction was north or imagine any maps. Everything was numb and she couldn't make sense of the light and noise and texture around her. She could hear herself screaming in the dark classroom, but it was as though the voice was not hers.

Then she was on her feet, Miss Robinson's hard hand seized upon her arm, pulling her for the door, out of the classroom and into the corridor. The door slammed, cutting out the laughter of the children inside. The lights returned. Dana was gasping for breath. Miss Robinson manoeuvred her over to the benches where the coats hung. "Sit down and take deep breaths."

"I'm going to die!" As Dana breathed, she sensed the signals that had gone coming back, all apart from the wLAN. Through the window on the classroom door, she saw the light on it had gone out, a plume of thin smoke dribbling up to pool on the ceiling.

Miss Robinson crouched so her head was level with Dana's. Dana could see all the lines at the edges of her mouth that her lipstick had run into. "Dana, I am a qualified first-aider. You're not going to die. You're just panicking and breathing wrong. The bang must have frightened you. It's a normal reaction."

Something about the way she used the word *normal* sent a pang of disgust leaping up from Dana's stomach. She got to her feet. "I know you told Pauline you think I do it on purpose, and it's my fault no-one likes me!"

Dana pushed Miss Robinson away and ran to the girls' lavatories. She went into a cubicle, slammed the door, and shot the bolt across. A moment later came the creak of the door opening. Miss Robinson's heels echoed and rang in the tiled room. "Dana?"

Dana said nothing.

"Dana?" Knuckles rapped and the door trembled against the thin metal bolt that kept the world out. "Open this door."

"No!" said Dana. "Piss off!"

"Okay, Dana," said Miss Robinson, and it sounded as though she was trying very hard to keep her voice calm. "I'm going to forget you just swore at me. I'm going to give you some time to calm down. When you feel better, come back to the classroom and we'll talk about what's going on over break."

The sound of Miss Robinson's shoes receded. A shuddering sob escaped Dana as soon as the main door closed. She took the fuse out of her pocket. The little silvery cylinder blurred in her palm when she looked at it.

The bell rang and girls clattered about the toilet cubicles outside the thin walls protecting her from them, turning taps and talking and flushing and banging. Dana didn't want to go outside for break and she didn't want to go back to Miss Robinson's class. People always said they would sort things out, that things would get better, but they never did. They never had done at any of the home she and Cale had before Pauline and Graeme fostered them, and they wouldn't work out in this school, either. Perhaps it *was* her fault nobody liked her. She stood in the cubicle with the door shut and tried very hard not to cry. She breathed for several minutes until she felt well enough to go out.

She was washing her hands when someone shouted, "Oi, Dictionary girl!" A forced tittering came from near the window.

Dana turned. Abigail emerged from a toilet cubicle. Her two henchgirls watched. Dana reached back and gripped the edge of the handbasin.

"No wonder your real parents didn't want a freak like you and that stupid, window-licking brother of yours who has to go to a *special* school."

A prickling heat crawled up Dana's neck. "Cale is not stupid."

"Not stupid compared to you," Abigail moved forward.

"Don't stand so close to me."

"I'll do what I like, you little runt!" Abigail thrust her face into Dana's, so close Dana could see the pores on her nose. Her breath stank of onion crisps. "I bet they paid social services to take you away!"

Dana's heart pounded, the surface of the basin

clammy under her hands. She desperately wanted to push Abigail's ugly great face away and run. Abigail grabbed a handful of Dana's jersey, yanking her away from the basin. Dana struck out, her hand connecting with a bone-jarring smack. Abigail lurched back with a howl, hair flying.

Another girl blocked the exit, leaning forward with her arms reached out like a goalkeeper in a football match. Dana pulled a plastic box away from the wall, scattering paper hand towels. She raised the box with both hands, trying to bring its sharp corner down on the girl's head.

A hand seized Dana's forearm. The towel box slipped from her grasp and hit the tiles. Dana caught sight of Abigail, blood spraying from her nose, eyes livid, the room spinning around them both. Dana unbalanced backwards, flinging out her arms in search of something for support and finding nothing. Her head wrenched forward on her neck and pain exploded into her skull. The air reverberated with a deafening ringing like a great porcelain bell.

Strange voices uttered distorted syllables. Dana sensed motion and hands on herself. Opening her eyes, she saw only unfocused patches of light. "Get off me!" she screamed, but when she tried to move, her neck felt caught up in something. A sharp pain pierced the inside of her elbow, and a dreadful pressure under her skin started up there. The voices faded to a distant murmur and her vision drifted out of focus.

-3-

D**ANA** sensed muffled noises and jolts of motion, but it was as though through the fabric of something else. She began to sense other things. Sudden flashes, at a frequency too great for her to count, which formed pictures and long Latin words in her head, and a noise that started out like the dial tone on a telephone with a number keyed into it, becoming a dull screech, then a squawking babble, and a rising wall of static. She wasn't sure if these things were real, or part of a dream, a product of her imagination.

She felt a mattress under her back. The repetitive beeping in her ears was real, coming from the machine by her bed. A fierce disinfectant smell choked her throat, and when she looked at her surroundings she saw a lurid curtain and horrid pictures of *Winnie the Pooh* characters stuck to the walls, and their colours were too strong. Dana lurched upright, doubling up as sick forced its way out and onto the sheet, the burning dampness soaking through to touch her skin.

Still retching, Dana flung the covers away. A man came through the curtains — it was Graeme. "Too much colour, too much colour," she spluttered at him. The surroundings passed in a blur as he moved her past the curtain and through a door.

Behind the door lay plain white. A sharp snap as Graeme turned off the lights, and the white room subdued itself. "Dana, calm down," said Graeme, and he knelt and held her to him. She had stopped retching and her breath came in uneven gasps.

"I keep seeing telephones dialling," she sobbed. "And hearing pictures."

"It's okay," Graeme reassured her. "The ambulance

man gave you a medicine to calm you down because you were having a fit. You've probably just reacted funny to it."

"What ambulance man?"

"Do you remember that some girls attacked you in the toilet?"

"Yes. It was Abigail. They tried to stop me from leaving, and she was saying things, so I hit her to make her stop and she pushed me over."

"When you fell, you hit your head on a basin, hard. So hard, the basin cracked and you knocked yourself out. You have a head injury the doctors call concussion. We're in a hospital now. The school called my work number to tell me there'd been an accident."

Dana was starting to make sense of her surroundings. She was in a toilet. Yes, this was a hospital. She could find it on her imaginary maps. It was called Coventry General Accident and Emergency Department, and it was about 24 miles from Pauline and Graeme's house. Graeme had vomit on his jersey, and she was wearing an oversized dress made of a plasticky material instead of her usual clothes. The clammy sticking sensation of the bare skin of her thighs touching underneath it was repellent. Cold air poked her skin through holes in the back.

"Do you think you can go back yet?" Graeme asked her. "I'm not really supposed to be in the ladies' loo."

Dana nodded. Graeme stood up and led her back through a corridor of curtains to the bed she'd been allocated.

A nurse in a blue uniform was removing the sheets. The smells of sick and disinfectant were very strong. The nurse smiled at Dana as she hefted the bedding into a large hopper and pushed it away.

"Pauline is fetching some of your things from home," Graeme explained. "Some doctors are coming to look at you."

A black man wearing a green tie stepped around the edge of the curtain. Another man with light-brown curly hair and round spectacles followed him. The second man drew his eyebrows down. "It stinks in here."

"I was sick," Dana apologised.

"I am the consultant, Mr Harris," said the first man. "And this is Dr Osric, a medical research scientist."

"Hello," said Dr Osric to Graeme. "Do you mind if I just examine her head?"

Graeme spoke to Dana. "Dr Osric is just going to spend a minute looking at you. You are okay with that, aren't you?"

"Yes."

Dana sat on the bed and Dr Osric put his hands on the sides of her head. Dana tried not to look at him as it made her feel awkward, especially with people she didn't know, but Dr Osric didn't seem to be looking at her, not in the way people usually did. He moved her forelock and studied the skin above her eyebrows, pressing with his thumbs. He started moving her hair around, apparently trying to look at her scalp. After repeating this, he shook his head. "I can't see any evidence of scarring."

He turned to Graeme. "You say this is your foster child. Were you told anything about her birth parents?"

Graeme shook his head. "Dana and her fraternal twin Cale were given up for adoption as babies. They don't remember anything about their birth parents, and the identity of those parents is protected."

"Nevertheless, the medical histories of the children should have been given, and some genetic history of the parents. With your consent, I'd like to make the relevant enquiries to see what information was recorded."

Graeme frowned. "All right. You'll have to check with social services."

When Dr Osric had gone, Dana asked if she could have her clothes back. She hated the loose hospital gown and the feel of only having her knickers on underneath it.

"I don't see why not," Mr Harris said. "Because you lost consciousness and you've been sick, we'd like to keep you in overnight for observation, but we'll put you in a private room in the paediatrics ward, and your foster parents can bring in your pyjamas."

"What were they saying about finding my real parents?" Dana asked Graeme when Mr Harris had gone.

Graeme took a seat on the bed next to Dana. "The doctors didn't know whether to tell you this or not. They did some scans of your head, to make sure you hadn't fractured your skull and that your brain wasn't bleeding, and they could see what looks like a piece of metal inside."

Dana stared at him. "Why is there a piece of metal in my head?"

"There's probably a very simple explanation for it. The bone at the front of your head might have been broken when you were too young to remember, and another doctor put in a piece of metal to mend it. That's why the doctors want to find out who your birth parents were, so they can find out why it was put there."

"Will I get to see my birth parents?"

Graeme hesitated. "Dana, there is probably a good reason why your parents gave you and Cale up for adoption."

"Because we have autism?"

"No, not at all because of that. It might have been that your dad left your mum alone with you, and she couldn't cope or she didn't have enough money. Or maybe they were ill. It might even be they died and didn't have any relatives to care for you. It might not even have been by choice. Some children are taken into care by court order because a judge decides how their birth parents are living is just not safe for them. Whyever it happened, everyone involved probably thought very hard about it first."

"Well, I'll be able to ask them, won't I? When they come."

"No. I'm sorry." Graeme paused. "You aren't allowed to look for your parents until you're eighteen, if you do decide to, and even then you might find out they don't want to be traced. You must understand the doctors are only looking this up to find out medical histories, not identities."

Dana nodded silently.

A nurse entered the cubicle with a wheelchair and a blanket. She smiled at Dana. "We've got a room for you in paediatrics. Would you like to come with me?"

The room was similar to an office, with aluminium Venetian blinds screening the windows from the corridor and a bed, table, and chair. Pauline turned up with a bag containing Dana's clothes and pyjamas. Pauline told Dana she needed to settle down and rest, and then she and Graeme left.

Dana knelt on the bed facing the window and peered through the blinds into the corridor, where Pauline and Graeme stood speaking. She couldn't hear them, but they didn't look very happy, and she wondered if they were arguing.

She looked down to the other end of the corridor where two men in white coats conversed, one black with a green tie and the other white with no tie, and she from this recognised them as Mr Harris and Dr Osric whom she'd met earlier. Dr Osric had a small computer in his hand, which he was tapping with a stylus. As Dana concentrated on the computer, an orange light at the top of it began to flicker, and the words Dr Osric's mouth was forming began to take on sounds.

"Provine, Dana and Caleb. Found abandoned. Caleb and Dana were the first names of the police officers on duty when they were brought in. They were given the last name 'Provine' from the initials of their finder, Mr P. R. Orange, and the name of the location, Vine Street. DNA confirmed they were fraternal twins, but failed to match them to any missing child cases. It was the 3rd of June and they were estimated to be about six months old."

"So nothing can be known of their parents' medical history," Mr Harris said.

Dr Osric continued. "There is no mention of any scarring on Dana's head or any other abnormalities noted at the time of their initial medical examination. I don't see how the object could have been put into her brain at another time. It's situated in the frontal lobe between the hemispheres. To get it there would mean removing the skin from the forehead and cutting away a segment of the skull. I can see no signs of bone healing or scarring to the skin."

Mr Harris glanced at the computer before speaking. "This was done when she was very young?"

"Even if it was done immediately after she was born, there would be evidence still where the bone has healed. Yet there is none."

"What are you saying?" said Mr Harris. "I've heard of deposits bioaccumulating in brains before, but this object appears to be some kind of electronic device."

Dana shivered, rattling the blinds with unsteady fingers.

"The object is small. There is a possibility, albeit a very slight one, that it was put into her brain *in utero*."

Mr Harris slowly shook his head. "That's *impossible*."

"I have to contact someone about this. I'll find you later. Don't speak to anyone else. This must not be leaked to the press."

Dr Osric turned away. He stopped mid-stride and took his computer back out. He looked at it in a puzzled way and tapped the screen with his stylus. Its signal disappeared from Dana's mind. Then Dr Osric looked directly at Dana where she was peering through the blinds. Their eyes locked. Dana took in breath sharply and pulled her fingers back. The blinds snapped closed, concealing her from Dr Osric.

She sat back on her bed, wrapping her arms around herself and rocking back and forth. Dana thought of all the days her foster families had always celebrated as her birthday, the 17th of February. From what she'd just heard, the 17th of February was a guess, just as likely to be her birthday as any day in February. Or March, or January. There was a device stuck in her brain and her real parents had dumped her and Cale in a place called Vine Street, and her name, Provine, which she had always thought was her one trace to who she really was, was just a fake, made-up one. She recalled hours spent looking through telephone directories, looking for the Provines, wondering if any of them were her parents. Provine was a Scottish name, so she'd often wondered if her real parents came from Scotland. They didn't. Her real mum was probably a dirty lady who slept in doorways and under bridges, who took heroin or whatever it was the drug addicts used to ruin their lives and their bodies, who hadn't even known her father properly, and had abandoned her and Cale in Vine Street. An image of tendril-throttled masonry wandered through Dana's mind. Vine Street.

She knelt up and looked through the blinds once more. Mr Harris was talking to Graeme and Pauline. Pauline was nodding her head vigorously, while Graeme stood still, gesticulating with his hands every so often. Eventually, Dr Harris left and Graeme and Pauline came in to Dana's room.

"Are you okay?" Graeme asked.

"My head still hurts."

"Pauline and I are just going to the café to have a cup of tea."

"Graeme," said Dana as he reached for the door. "Am I a proper person?"

Graeme came back in and closed the door. "Of course you are." He sat down on the bed next to her. "Autistic isn't wrong; just different."

Dana wiped tears away from her eyes. "No, I mean because there's a metal thing in my head. Robots and computers are made from metal, not people."

"Oh, *Dana*," Pauline said, and she wiped her eyes and turned away.

"Lots of people have bits of metal in them. Duncan broke his leg when he was little and they had to put in a metal pin to fix the bone back together. My great uncle Fred was in the army and his leg blew off when he trod on a mine. He had to have a fake leg. He used to stick fridge magnets on his trousers and walk around."

Dana tried to force herself to laugh, but it came out as more of a sobbing noise.

"And some of my teeth have metal fillings in them,

look." Graeme opened his mouth.

"I want to go home, Graeme."

"You can come home tomorrow, I promise. The doctors just want you to stay here tonight, so they can be sure you're okay."

"I don't want to go back to that—" a shuddering gulp made Dana break off "—school!"

"I know you had a bad time there today, but what happened was an accident, and it will get easier if you give it a chance."

"No, Graeme, I don't want to go back there! Ever!"

"When you're feeling better, then, we'll talk about it with the headteacher and the social worker."

Dana sniffed. "Are they going to take the bit of metal out?"

"Probably not. It'd cause more trouble than to leave it there. It's not doing you any harm." Graeme rummaged in his pocket. "Here. I've brought you a fuse."

Dana studied the fuse, which had black writing on it. "Two amps."

"It broke in my lamp at work today."

"Thank you, Graeme."

⧖

Dana lay propped up in bed in her hospital room, holding the two-amp fuse. Graeme and Pauline had gone home an hour ago, saying they would come back for her in the morning.

Meaningless data streamed from the wLAN in the corridor, where doctors and nurses walked back and forth. She'd eaten her dinner: soggy courgettes and broccoli with mashed potatoes and flavourless meat, bathed in watery gravy. The nurse who brought it had found Dana sitting in there with the light off and gasped, and asked her why she was sitting in the dark. Dana hated the stark lights in the hospital; they made her eyes hurt.

Through the window in her room glowed the many lights of the city. As Dana slipped into the vacuous space between sleep and wake, she became aware of a distant whisper whose words she couldn't quite make out. Blurry colours flickered on the insides of her eyelids. The horizon to the north had an odd tinge to it.

Dana sat up. The sensation felt like a promise, a reassurance. If she could get to whatever was sending her that signal, she would be safe. In the place where that feeling came from, she wouldn't have to go to a school. It wouldn't matter about a piece of metal being in her head.

She stuffed clothes into her school bag and went out to the corridor, squinting down at the floor so the light was not so strong.

"Dana, where are you going?" said a gentle voice.

Dana looked up at a smiling nurse. "I want to go to the toilet."

The nurse led her to the lavatory. "I'll come back in a minute to check you're okay."

Dana hastily got dressed. When she came out, the nurse had gone. The door to the stairs had a thing beside it for swipecards, and it unlocked when Dana told it to. She went down two floors and through a door marked *staff only*. Metal trolleys stood in a corridor, some bearing scissors and knives and other tools she couldn't identify. Dana put her hand in her pocket and held her fuse tightly. She continued to the end of the corridor, where two sets of doors led to the rear exit.

The air was sharp and refreshing after the smells in the hospital. She fastened her coat against the cold of the night. Stars shone in the clear sky. Big dustbins on wheels towered over her, edging a path leading along the wall of the building. Dana stumbled on cracks in the concrete path she couldn't see in the shadows. She sensed a signal from a CCTV camera and saw an image of herself in her mind, wandering along in an odd black and white, a small figure with shiny reflective eyes.

Light reflected upon a puddle obstructing the pavement by the corner of the building ahead. Dana scrambled up a bank of stones and sparse grass rising behind the angle of the path. The ground fell away on the other side to a copse of stunted trees and a wire fence.

The lights of the roads and the dark horizon stretched away into the distance. Bright stars faded into the haze of light to the east where the city lay. North was where she had sensed *it*. When she turned her head, Dana saw colours and shapes in her peripheral vision. The faint sound intensified in the ear facing them, but when she looked directly at the place they had been, she saw nothing.

Dana shivered. Another image took form in her mind. A figure wearing a long coat stood in shadow, the same black and white as she had seen herself in before. It watched something, as a cat watches a bird. The head turned, and a woman's face looked straight at her, pale and solemn with dark eyes. The woman slipped away, out of the picture.

Dana stared into the shadow at the foot of the building. She slithered back down the bank as quietly as she could. Her eyes couldn't penetrate the darkness, and the only other thing she could discern was the empty image of concrete path and brick wall where the woman had just been.

Dana leaned forward into the shadow and listened. Every sense in her strained for purchase, but all she found was the distant noise of traffic and the chill draught emanating from the passage. The darkness stood like a wall.

In the silence of her concentration, the faint whispering began again. Dana turned back to look up the bank.

A foot scraped on the concrete. As Dana turned, the taller form of an adult collided with her, pinning her arms against her sides.

"Let go!" Dana shouted, kicking, sending a spray of water up from the puddle on the concrete as the assailant spun her around. Fierce eyes scrutinised her face.

"Are you Dana?"

There was nothing friendly about this woman. Her grip hurt and her question was a demand. "Yes!"

The woman's shoulders sagged, but she did not let

go of Dana. She raised her face to the night sky, as if searching there for the answer to an unasked question.

"So he did go through with it," she said at last.

$$-4-$$

DANA shouted out and struggled against the woman as she dragged her down steps leading along the wall of the building to a car park. Although the windows in the hospital were lit, she saw no-one within.

The woman wrenched open a door to a car with dark paint — Dana couldn't see what colour — and manhandled Dana inside. The door slammed behind her and Dana at once turned and tried to open it. Although the knob at the bottom of the window was up, the handle didn't work.

Dana screamed as loudly as she could the moment the woman opened the driver's door. The woman twisted to look over the back of her seat. "Stop making that awful noise and put your seatbelt on." As she spoke, she took a pair of spectacles with round, dark-tinted lenses from the inside pocket of her coat and put them on.

The car started with a shudder though its chassis and a coarse diesel roar. The woman pulled away with a force that pushed Dana firmly down into her seat. Dana scrambled over and pulled hard at the door handle on the other side.

"I would not bother with that if I were you," the woman said. "The rear doors of this vehicle are fitted with a purely mechanical device they used to call a childlock."

The car had reached the turnoff out of the hospital onto the main road. The woman pushed the indicator, looked left once, and the car turned right. In desperation, Dana stood up and reached forward, trying to scratch the woman in the eye. Without even turning, the woman got hold of Dana's wrist and twisted her arm down between the seats.

"Sit still before I make you sit still!" She released Dana's arm in order to change gear.

Wind shrilled through the open window, but the gap was too narrow to try to escape through. Dana sat back in the seat and watched the passing traffic. No police cars; not much traffic at all. Dana knew what this woman was: she was a *stranger*. No matter with whom she and Cale had lived, this much had been drilled into her. Do not take sweets if a stranger offers you them. Do not get into a car with a stranger. Strangers took children away and murdered them, left their bodies rotting in woods. She had seen it on the news.

Traffic lights glowed green ahead. *You can't go past a red light*, Dana thought, and she concentrated on the lights. The light turned to red. The woman put her foot down and the car surged forward.

"For future reference, traffic lights do not change from green to red without going orange first."

The car arrived at a large roundabout and turned onto dual carriageway. The woman indicated and pulled out into the right-hand lane. The needle on the speed gauge rose to 80 mph. She pressed something on the dashboard. A map lit up, like a section of the ones Dana could imagine if she tried. The woman took something from the seat next to her — a mobile telephone — and pressed a key and spoke into it.

"Osric?"

She listened.

"Yes. Look, Rupert, there are some cameras on the east side of the building. I want whatever they recorded disposed of." She put down the telephone.

"It's illegal to use a telephone while you're driving," said Dana, "and it's illegal to go faster than seventy miles an hour on this road."

A green arrow-shaped light on the dashboard flashed. Now the car was turning off the dual carriageway, tearing down a wide road, turning several times before stopping in a narrow lane with a stony, potholed surface.

The woman switched off the engine and leaned back heavily in her seat. She gripped the top of the steering wheel with one hand and let off a loud, angry exhalation.

"Well, Dana, my name is Jananin Blake. Though it's highly unlikely I ever met your father, or the woman who gave birth to you, it seems I am, genetically, your mother."

Dana stared at the woman. She had shoulder-length, very dark hair, of the same thick wavy texture as Cale's and, she supposed, her own.

"If you're my mother," she said, after a long pause, "why did you leave me on Vine Street? And if you didn't want me then, why do you want me now?"

"I didn't leave you on Vine Street." Jananin Blake looked at her watch. "Four hours ago, I didn't even know you existed."

Vine Street. Mr P. R. Orange. Dana and Cale the police officers on duty that night. The failed adoption. The succession of foster carers. The school, the toilet, the hospital. How could a mother not know, not be there, for all that time? Dana became aware of tears running down her own face. Jananin Blake did not reach out to her like Pauline and Graeme and the other adults who had looked after Dana had; rather, she retracted and frowned.

Dana was breathing hard, and her next words came out as a shouted demand. "If you're my mother, why is there a piece of metal in my head?"

For a long time, Jananin Blake gave no answer.

"This will be hard for you to understand, but I see no sense in lying."

The woman looked out the window at the dark trees. Behind the gnarled and leafless hedge the eyes of some nocturnal creature glinted in the headlamps.

"You exist because Ivor Pilgrennon took something I invented and used it for a purpose I did not authorise, and then he stole my gametes — eggs, I suppose —

and used them to make a child. And you have a radio transceiver device in your brain because Ivor Pilgrennon put it there."

-5-

THE noise and light of curtains being pulled back woke Dana. Jananin Blake stood before a window in the thin light of morning, a steaming mug in one hand.

"You talk in your sleep. There is food and tea on the table if you want it."

"I talk?" Dana squinted, trying to recall what had been going through her head while she slept. "About what?"

"It sounded like a telephone conversation with someone called Gamma."

The headache from the basin in the school toilet was gone. Jananin had driven on into the night, and Dana had asked questions, though the answers confused her and she recalled little beyond Jananin's initial revelation. She remembered vaguely their arrival late at night, of an instruction not to draw attention to herself and of creeping upstairs and falling asleep on the sofa of the room she was now in.

Jananin watched something through the window. In the light of day, she looked to be in her late thirties. Her hair had begun to grey at the temples. She had a lean, muscular build, as Dana supposed a woman of this age who hadn't given birth might. She wore boots and close-fitting thick trousers, and what appeared to be a long knife in a leather sheath was strapped to her left thigh.

Dana poured the teapot into a mug. The weight of it in her hand made it dribble over the toast and over the side of the tray. She imagined a map, locating her position some distance off the M1 motorway past the Derby turnoff and east of Stoke on Trent. "Where are we?"

"It's a Bed and Breakfast."

"Is this where you live?" If Jananin was Dana's mother as she claimed, Dana wasn't sure what was supposed to happen next. Would she have to live with her, as she had with the succession of foster carers she'd moved between prior to her and Cale being placed with Pauline and Graeme? What about Cale? They'd always been together, at least in terms of who they lived with, if not at school. "Have I got to stay here now?"

Jananin Blake shook her head. "I was hoping you might be able to help me find Ivor Pilgrennon."

"I don't know where he is, and I don't think I'd be much help. You probably wouldn't want me when you find out what I'm like. I've lived with different foster parents and none of them worked. I've got autism, you see."

Jananin stared at Dana. "It's Pilgrennon's fault you have autism."

"Graeme says autism isn't a disease, and you can't catch it off other people."

"It's a genetic condition. It can be passed on from your parents. I have it as well, or something like it. Years ago, it was called Asperger's syndrome. That's why Pilgrennon went to such lengths to steal my ova. He wanted to make autistic children and implant devices in them, so they could interface to computers, to prove a theory he had."

Dana didn't know what to say in response to this. Jananin continued.

"It's highly likely Pilgrennon has a signal emitter, a beacon of a sort, wherever he is hiding. He would have intended it so that you or any other of his creatures he's managed to lose can sense it and find him, but not me or anyone else who might be looking. If that is so, you may be able to lead me to that beacon."

Dana stared about the room, at the sofa she was sitting on. "But if I go off with you and don't tell anyone,

Pauline and Graeme will wonder where I am. If I come with you to look for Pil... thingy..." Her voice trailed off.

Something had occurred to her. Dana was the one who had left the hospital. It had been she who had not wanted to face the doctors, and the school, and Pauline and Graeme again. She did not know Jananin Blake, but Jananin Blake was now presenting her with an escape.

"If I go with you, will I have to go to a school?"

"No."

Dana stared up at Jananin Blake, taking in her proud posture, the hardness of her expression. "You can drive a car. Have you got, like, a job, and a house, or do you live with your parents or in sheltered accommodation?"

"I live in a house, which I own," said Jananin. "And I used to have a job."

"Did you get sacked from the job, because you have autism?"

"No. I still do have it, I suppose, although my role is more consultancy-based and part-time, these days."

Dana watched her a little longer. Jananin didn't talk down to her, try to simplify what she said, like Miss Robinson did. And like Pauline and Graeme and other adults sometimes did.

"Do you think, when I'm older, I could have a job, and drive a car, and live in a house that I own?"

Jananin scrutinised Dana for a moment. She raised her eyebrows. "I don't see why not. Do you not want to do those things?"

"I do, it's just..." It had been a social worker at the last foster home she'd been in. She had lectured at length about how it was important to have *realistic expectations*. She had gone through what it was like to live in sheltered accommodation rented out by the council, where Dana would have a bedroom to herself but share a kitchen and communal facilities, and that if Dana worked very hard, she might be able to aspire to a job picking up litter, or putting people's shopping in a bag, or other employment of that sort.

"What do you need me to do?"

"I'm not entirely sure, yet. Pilgrennon has links both to rural Wales and Scotland. I've travelled to both in search of him, but found no trace. You may have the ability to find him, so our best bet is to head either north or west. Perhaps it will become clearer how to pick up the trail when we are somewhere a trail is likely to be found."

Dana quickly finished breakfast. After she'd had a shower and cleaned her teeth in the small *en-suite*, she found Jananin tidying the room. A laptop computer lay on the bed. The screen showed a bad drawing of an owl — just a shape with wings drawn on and a face — carrying a white flower in its claws, within an email from Rupert Osric. Dana remembered that name: the doctor in the hospital from yesterday. The same person Jananin had spoken to on her mobile telephone.

Jananin put on a brown leather trench coat with a heavy collar, which concealed the knife attached to her leg. "Now, if you are coming with me, we have to leave here with the minimum commotion. Not least because if they notice that mess you made with the tea, I'll probably be charged for it." Jananin put on her dark glasses and counted some bank notes. "Walk ahead of me, go out the door, and stand by the car. Don't look back or stop."

Dana didn't look at the desk as she went downstairs; she couldn't see or sense signals from any cameras. Behind her, Jananin placed the keys and money on the counter and thanked whoever stood behind it.

A few red and gold leaves still clung to the branches of the trees about the car park, bristling with crystalline frost hairs left by the cold night. Dana stood by the old dark-silver car, studying the glassy, metallic recesses of its headlamps. Jananin hefted up the boot door to sling her luggage in. A curved object a few feet long lay inside, looking like it was made of black plastic at first glance. Straps of dark leather formed an interlacing pattern on the handle.

"What's that?" As Dana tried to comprehend it, she realised it wasn't plastic, but glossy lacquer of the traditional sort made in the far East, etched with intricate gold figures, perhaps words in another language, and that the lacquer was a scabbard, and the handle was the only visible part of what was inside it. "Is that a Samurai sword?"

"Yes, a katana."

"Why do you need a Samurai sword?"

"I need a weapon that cannot be affected by computers."

"It's illegal to carry knives and swords around. Either in your car boot or tied to your leg."

Jananin frowned. "I don't take it with me when I go shopping, if that's what you're thinking. Although sometimes when there's a sale on, I perhaps wish I did. When Rupert Osric told me there was a child at Coventry General with an autism diagnosis and a device wedged between her frontal lobes, I feared the worst. Pilgrennon himself could have been there. I had to be prepared for all eventualities."

"Can I look at it?"

"No, you can't." Jananin closed the boot door. "The Samurai had a saying: the wise give life with the sword; the fool kills himself on another's sword."

She unlocked the passenger door and opened it for Dana.

"Ivor Pilgrennon was a psychologist," Jananin began as she drove. "He ran a research institute in Oxford, studying autistic children. He theorised that people with autism were much better at understanding computers than ordinary people, because of the way their minds worked. When he stole my ova, Rupert Osric and I found out he was experimenting with *in vitro* embryos with the intention of making autistic foetuses. Research that violates international ethics standards. In short, eugenics."

"What do you mean when you say *ova*? People don't lay eggs. They have periods and sex and women get pregnant. They make us draw diagrams of it at school."

"Female humans have *ova*, which are the equivalent and what would become eggs in animals that lay eggs."

Dana frowned. "What, like frogspawn?"

"We located what I believe to be the surrogate he was using, but she lied to us about her involvement with him. We had no inkling, at that time, that his research had progressed to implanting and gestating embryos to the point of live birth. We gathered sufficient evidence to expose Pilgrennon and report him to the police for his illegal research, but he set off a device called a Compton bomb that none of us suspected he had. It destroyed his research institute and released a signal that overloaded electronic devices for miles around. Pilgrennon escaped in the chaos. I have no doubt Pilgrennon is prepared to use a Compton bomb again if he feels threatened. It would destroy any electrical things near it, including you."

"What? How?" Dana wasn't sure she wanted to hear this.

"Osric copied me that scan of your head. The position of the device means that if it overloaded, it would burn away the parts of your brain that control your higher functions. Even if you were to survive, you would be little more than a breathing corpse."

"Then *why* are we going to look for him?" An image had formed in Dana's mind: a sly James Bond villain sitting in a swivel chair behind a sickle-shaped metal desk, his finger hovering over a red button that would end everything, and make her — what was it Jananin Blake said — a breathing corpse, with smoke coming out of her ears.

"Because if we do not, it's likely he may look for you in order to destroy you, should he ever learn of your existence. He may well be regretting what he did in his past now. If Pilgrennon ever wants to get back to the respectable research community, he will have to first exonerate himself, and that means getting rid of any surviving evidence of his deeds."

Dana didn't want to know about this sinister Pilgrennon or where she had come from any more. She wanted to go back to Pauline and Graeme's house. Perhaps they wouldn't make her go to the school again.

Jananin knocked her hand against the roof of the car, making Dana jump. "However, we've learnt from Pilgrennon. This car runs on diesel, so there are no spark plugs to be affected. The chassis is covered in a polymer alloy I invented. It's impervious to Compton radiation." Jananin reached down and turned the handle on the inside of the door, and the gap in the window closed. An image and Dana's sensation of the car's position on the M1 disappeared from the back of her mind.

"I can't think of maps any more when you do that!"

Jananin opened the window again and reached across to switch on the device on the dashboard. The screen lit up to show a map like the one Dana could imagine. "Maps like this?"

"Yes. Is that... Can other people not see those too?"

"No. This computer uses its own software to interpret signals from satellites that orbit the Earth. It's a technique called GPS. It would seem you are able to receive GPS signals and have learnt to interpret them."

"Jananin, can you tell which way is north?"

"I can from that." Jananin waved her hand at the computer. "Or if the sun is in the sky and I know what time of day it is, I can calculate it."

"I mean, if you shut your eyes and spun round, would you be able to tell?"

"No."

Dana looked at her feet and the bits of dirt trapped in the rubber mat in the seatwell. Her vision blurred.

Even other people who have autism, it seemed, were not like her.

She sensed Jananin Blake turn her head to look at her. "It would be useful to me if I could tell which direction was north always, and read maps without a computer. I would consider it an advantage."

Dana blinked and tried to think about something else. "What was it you said the car is covered with, that stops the GPS and the Compton bombs from getting in?"

"Polymer alloy. They're a class of compounds I invented. Some people called them 'intelligent materials' or 'programmable matter' but that's a load of gimmickmongering rubbish. If you arrange metal atoms inside chains of non-metal atoms in specific ways, you can combine the properties of polymers and metals. For example, the windows on this car. They let light in, but they conduct electricity. It's a similar idea with the molecules Pilgrennon stole from me that connect the device in your head to the neurons in your brain. They let current pass from one neuron to one receptor, but they're made from the same stuff as your DNA, so they can make more of themselves, so you can have lots of connections."

"Oh." Dana didn't understand. She looked out the window at the passing fields, drab polygons of brown and green against the overcast winter sky.

"I think I might like your GPS better than the annoying woman on my SatNav." Jananin glanced at the device on the dashboard. "In order to get to the main road towards Glasgow from here, I believe there are two basic possible routes. What are they and which is the most direct?"

Dana wound down the window a crack, then wound it back up again. "Stay on the M1 until Leeds and then go to the A65 to the M6."

At Penrith they stopped. Dana was hungry and needed the loo. Jananin told her to go to the toilets in the service station alone and to wait by the car.

The service station was an exposed place on a wet and windy day. The only people about were truckers, smoking behind their lorries in the car park or sitting alone at tables drinking coffee or eating sandwiches. The ladies' toilets were empty. Dana considered that had she not come with Jananin, she would be in school right now and running the gauntlet of lunchtime break.

Instead, she enjoyed the loneliness of the service-station toilet free of the menace of people like Abigail as she washed and dried her hands. As Dana walked back to the car, head bent and hood pulled up against the weather, something arrested her attention through a window looking in on an American fast-food kiosk.

Graeme?

It was Graeme, on the screen of the television up in the corner above the counter. He was sitting at a desk with a microphone in front of him. A red BBC logo hovered above his left shoulder. His mouth moved. Dana concentrated, watching the screen.

...Dana is a clever, funny girl. She wasn't exactly popular at the school she'd recently started going to, but I and my wife and our son, and her brother, miss her very much. If someone knows where she is, we exhort you to tell the police. Graeme looked up at the camera and twisted his eyebrows. *Dana, if you're watching this, please come home.*

Graeme disappeared and a news reader replaced him.

And that was Graeme Ro-

As Dana passed the corner of the building, a hissing started in her ears and orangy colours burst in her vision. She spun to face north-north-west, where grey rain-soaked countryside spread.

A muffled bang, and the staff member at the fast food counter let out a shriek. Dana turned back to see a a blank screen where Graeme and the news reader had been and a stream of smoke drifting up from the television. She broke into a run, returning to the car as fast as she could, afraid it might be Pilgrennon setting off a Compton bomb. She pulled the door handle, but the car was locked and wouldn't open when she told it to.

Footsteps sounded behind her. "Get in the car," said Jananin, reaching past Dana to unlock the door. Jananin dumped a warm carrier bag in Dana's lap and pulled away before Dana had shut the door properly.

"Graeme was on the telly, talking about me. It's like what happened at the hospital, only stronger."

Jananin glanced at Dana. "What happened at the hospital?"

"*Something*. It came from the north. I thought it must be to do with the hospital. I've never noticed it before."

"That hospital is on a hill. It could be Pilgrennon's beacon." Jananin flexed her hands on the steering wheel. "We were too far south for you to have detected it before. If it came from the north, he must be in Scotland, not Wales."

"But it's like noise, and colour, and... and like when your face is near a fire and you can feel the heat."

"Yes, well, it's probably interfering with your sensory perception and inducing a kind of synaesthesia."

"Oh," said Dana. "What does that mean?"

"It means your different senses get confused."

"That's what I said." Dana pointed at the bag. "What's this?"

"It's a Chinese takeaway."

Not far away, Jananin pulled over into a layby on a quiet stretch of road. A small, hairy horse grazed on the other side of the gate. Little brown birds moved in the hedge.

"You say the signal comes from the north?"

"The north-north-west, at Penrith," said Dana, her mouth full of crispy duck.

"Do you like that?"

"Mm."

"Try to keep it in your mouth and in the container,

then, and not all over my car."

"Graeme used to do Chinese squid, but they made Cale fart."

"I'd rather you didn't do that in the car, either. Who's Cale?"

"My brother."

Jananin coughed and spat out her crispy duck. "Your foster brother, or your genetic brother?"

"My genetic brother, I think. The people at the hospital said I was found with him."

"Can he read GPS and make computers do things like you can?"

"No, he can't even turn the stereo on without the remote control. I tried to teach him but he'd rather think about beetles. I think he could do it, if he wanted to. But he prefers to observe." Dana thought of Cale, watching while she and Duncan played computer games.

Jananin put the duck back in her mouth and swallowed. "If Graeme was on the news, it means you must have been reported missing to the police."

"He was saying things about me. It was strange. It's like when you go to a cemetery and you read the writing on the stones."

"The epitaphs."

"It was like I was dead, and another person was reading the one about me."

"What did he say?"

"That I was clever and funny. I don't know what kind of funny he meant. Some people say I'm funny, and they don't mean something nice."

"He probably meant the other meaning, that you are humorous, then."

Dana put rice and sauce into one of the plastic dishes. "When will I see Graeme again?"

Jananin exhaled. "I am sorry I had to take you away, and I am sorry to cause your family stress. But you have to understand, Dana, that I really must find Pilgrennon and stop what he is doing. That way, you can go back to your family and live a normal life."

Dana glared at the white lines in the middle of the road and kicked the underside of the glove compartment. "I don't expect Cale and me will get to stay with Pauline and Graeme anyway. It never lasts and I never had a normal life."

Jananin looked at her sharply. "It's nothing compared to the life you'll have if it becomes known that you can break televisions and read maps you can't see."

"You're a scientist — like Pilgrennon — aren't you?"

"Yes. I used to be a researcher at Cambridge University. Until Pilgrennon stole my invention."

They had both finished drinking, so Jananin put the mugs, the carton, and the remains of the Chinese food in the carrier bag.

"If the signal comes from north-north-west, can you locate its actual position using GPS?"

"I don't know."

"Then wind down the window and try."

Dana opened the window. "No. It just comes from that direction. It's not on the GPS."

"All right, then. I'm going to keep going north."

"When you find Pilgrennon, what will you do?"

Jananin put one hand on top of the steering wheel. She exhaled forcefully through her nose and flexed her shoulders under the wide, heavy collar of her coat. "Kill him."

Dana wound the window back up as the car pulled away.

Soon after they crossed the Scottish border, the roads became tortuous. Jananin pulled off the motorway near Paisley. The soiled undergrowth that grew beside the dual carriageway was replaced by scrubby bushes and heathers that fell away in an undulating grey-green, devoid of trees save for thick copses of pine at the bases of massive, cloud-wreathed hills and the occasional naked specimen in the garden of a blank-windowed stone cottage. It got dark at three o'clock. The terrain became steeper, the roads climbing and winding around it. Sudden inclines at the edge of the road were marked only by small pillars striped with reflective paint and catseyes on the tops. Often there were no catseyes in the road, or they were so damaged and muddied as not to work.

As the car left the A82, a dark expanse of water with black crags protruding from it opened on the left. White surf showed around the bases of the rocks.

"Does the signal come from the west yet?" Jananin asked.

An icy wind blasted in when Dana opened the window.

"It's still more north than west."

Wind whined over the bonnet of the car, rocking the suspension. Jananin put her foot down and the car roared north-east up the A828. Dana soon saw more water, this time on the right of the car. She opened the window. Loch Ness. Jananin pulled off before they reached the end of it. Dana wondered if there was a monster, or if it was too dark to see it even if there were.

Dana half-slept, the distant gleam of small towns and the noises of the wind and the engine disturbing her dreams too much for her to lose herself in exhaustion.

At last the car slowed. She looked out the window to see the ground rising black against an empty sky. Jananin turned the steering wheel hard. The headlamps illuminated a muddy road, rocks lying either side of it. The car jolted forward on the broken surface, rearing against the gradient. The engine snarled, and the bouncing headlamps lit upon a stone wall. Jananin got the car back on to level ground and stopped before a dented garage door. She put the handbrake on and got out. In the instant the door was open, the wind tore inside, messing up Dana's hair and flinging a paper bag around the back seat.

The garage door made a metallic scream as Jananin lifted it, the wind blowing her hair and coat around. She got back into the car and drove it in.

Dana stood by the car while Jananin closed the garage door behind it. With the headlamps off, she could see nothing. She heard the rattle of keys and the scrape of a lock turning.

"Come round the front of the car. The door's on the right."

Heat radiated from the car's bonnet. The engine smelt and made *plink* noises. Spider webs brushed Dana's face and something clattered to the floor as she fumbled along the front wall.

Jananin's hand found her arm and pulled her through the doorway. She trod on uneven stone. The door closed and the wind howled. Jananin scrabbled for a moment, and a torch revealed a shabby kitchen with a gas cooker and fridge freezer.

"Where is the signal now?"

Dana turned from side to side. "North-west."

Jananin led her into a hallway, where the torch illuminated cobwebby banisters and a stag's head hanging on the wall. Dana shuddered. "Is this *your* house, Jananin?"

"Yes, I bought it a few years ago in a property auction. The previous owner died intestate with no living relatives. Most of his possessions are still in it."

Jananin led Dana up the stairs to a small bedroom. "You can sleep here. I think there are some clothes in this cupboard." She pulled the curtain across and found another torch lying on the bedside table, which she gave to Dana. "I'm going downstairs to turn the electricity back on."

Dana found some men's striped pyjamas in the wardrobe.

When Jananin came back and switched on the light,

she held them out and asked, "Can you cut the labels out, please?"

Jananin frowned. "I suppose so."

"They itch," Dana explained as Jananin went back downstairs. She came back with the pyjamas minus the labels. Dana inspected them. She had cut them close enough to the seams; often people cut them and left too much, making them itch even worse.

"Keep the curtains shut if the lights are on," said Jananin.

Dana got changed while Jananin was downstairs. The landing didn't look much better with the lights on. The wallpaper and panelling were bashed about through decades of wear, and thick cobwebs covered the corners. Dana went to the ajar door at the top of the stairs and pushed it open. She smelled mould. Her hand found a bathroom light switch. The tiles were cracked, the fittings old and discoloured. Black stuff hung out the taps on the sink. The shower dripped steadily, a stalactite of the same black stuff hanging from it. She went to the toilet and didn't wash her hands. She was about to get into bed when something else occurred to her.

Dana went onto the landing and leaned over the banister; she jumped back when it moved.

"Jananin!"

After a moment, Jananin appeared at the bottom of the stairs and peered up at her over the rims of her dark glasses. She had taken off her brown leather coat but the knife was still strapped to her thigh. "What?"

"Did the man who lived here before die in that bed?"

"No, he died in the room behind you, because it stinks of disinfectant in there and the carpet and bed are missing."

Dana turned sharply to face the door.

"Go to bed," said Jananin.

Dana lay in her musty-smelling bed and wondered about the dead man's ghost haunting the house. She imagined him being an old man with a beard, who wore a kilt and a deerstalker hat and hunted stags with a blunderbuss. The wind shrilled around the ancient stone house and made the roof timbers creak.

-6-

DANA leaned on the base of the window and stretched her head and shoulders out of the car. She pictured the device in her head as the needle in a compass, drawn to the source like a magnet to the pole.

"It's still west of here."

Five yards from the roadside the ground fell away. Beyond, a flat expanse of grey water stretched to the horizon, its surface a Spirograph of wind-torn ruffles. The faint whispers and glimpses of strange colour lay behind that horizon. The wind buffeted up the cliffside, tearing at Dana's hair and shaking the chassis of Jananin's car.

Jananin got out and walked around the car to stand on the grass, looking down at the sea. She glanced back at Dana and raised her voice against the wind. "Across the Minch lies the Isle of Lewis. That back there," she pointed to the mass of rocks and land jutting into the sea to the north, "is Skye."

Dana opened the car door and stepped over the muddy verge to stand beside Jananin. "What's *beyond* Lewis?"

"Greenland." Jananin turned her head to Dana. "Canada and America."

"What if Pilgrennon's beacon is in one of those?"

After a long pause, Jananin said, "No. You are receiving a directional signal. If the beacon was that far away, you wouldn't be able to detect it because of the curvature of the Earth from the point of transmission. The signal would fly off into space." Jananin curved the back of one hand and held the other one flat against it. She lowered her hands to her sides, her fists clenching. "He must be on Lewis."

Dana took a step onto the grass, and Jananin's hand landed on her shoulder. "Don't go any closer to the edge in this wind."

Dana imagined a map and studied the routes on it. "There is a ferry. GPS says. It goes from Ullapool to... Stor- Stor-nor-way. Stornoway, is that right?"

"I don't know."

"Jananin, what is a ferry?"

Jananin put her hands in her coat pockets and shifted her weight back onto her heels. "In this case it is a seagoing craft that transports cars and passengers. To go by ferry to one of the Scottish islands these days requires some form of identification. They will keep a record at the terminal of who has left. It's not so extreme it requires a passport, but it's no longer possible to go there and disappear, as Pilgrennon demonstrated. We cannot simply go to Lewis without questions being asked. I will have to think about this."

Jananin spoke little on the drive back. The sky cleared and the sun shone low over the windswept landscape, striking bright patches of snow up on the mountains' stony peaks.

"Jananin, when is a big hill a mountain?"

"I don't know."

Dana was used to adults not knowing.

"In Australia," she said, looking at the car clock, which read 12:01, "is it tomorrow or yesterday?"

Jananin glanced at the clock. "I think it's tomorrow. Why didn't you think about that when we were stopped?"

"I don't think it's on GPS." Dana opened the window. It wasn't. "The clock that tells me the time is called—" Dana paused, "—*Green witch*."

"*Grenitch*," Jananin corrected. "The Greenwich Atomic Clock."

Jananin left Dana in the living room of the old Inverness house. There was no television, and she could sense none of the other signals stereos and other electrical equipment tended to emit. There were shelves of old books, and a few vinyl records in coloured sleeves for a record player with an arm and a spindle under a yellowed plastic cover. The furniture was old and faded. Dana knelt on the sofa, facing backwards to the window, and found a porcelain figure standing on the windowsill, which she played with and broke. She put it back and hoped Jananin Blake wouldn't notice.

Beyond the flaky timbers that held the window together and the pale yellow wool of spider egg sacs gumming their crevices, dark conifers lined the slope down to a flat stretch of water: Loch Luichart. The trees continued to the mountainous horizon. Although she knew a railway line and the A832 ran along in front of the water from GPS, she could see no sign of human habitation anywhere. Graeme and Pauline would never have thought of looking here for her. The distant shape of a big bird circled lazily. Dana knew little about birds.

Dana passed some time reading a book about houseplants, which she found interesting because she had a couple of cacti on the windowsill at Pauline and Graeme's house. Gradually it became too dark to read, and she recalled Jananin's warning about switching on lights and put the book back.

She wandered upstairs and found Jananin kneeling on the floor in one of the rooms, beside a book with electronic diagrams in it. Spread out on the bed was an electronic device with the case opened and most of the components outside of it, but Dana couldn't tell what it was, or if Jananin was building it or dismantling it.

"What are you doing?"

"Working on an electronics project."

"What for?"

"None of your business."

Dana looked at a large poster stuck to the wall near the door. It showed different letters and numbers with full stops and hyphens below them.

"What's this?"

Jananin looked up. "It's Morse code."

"What's it for?"

"It's for sending messages. You send combinations of long and short signals to make up letters or numbers."

"Oh." Dana sat on the bed. "It's like how the computers talk."

"I suppose so. You must understand direct machine code."

"I don't know what that means."

"Believe me, you do. Better than I do."

Dana scrutinised a montage of illustrations of pale flowers with waxy petals. They were intricately detailed, some with drops of water on them. Each showed a different stage of the flower opening. "Cale can draw like this. Only things he can see."

In the kitchen, Dana sat on a stool while Jananin prepared a curry of smoked fish and eggs with rice.

Jananin pointed to a small television perched on the fridge. "Put it on BBC1, the news is starting."

Dana looked at the television. The picture lit up to show a newsreader talking about cabinet ministers.

The scents of cardamom and turmeric filled the shabby kitchen, making it feel more a house where people lived than an empty shell whose owner had died and gone. "What are you going to do about Pilgrennon?"

Jananin stirred the food. "I had always assumed someone would be concealing Pilgrennon, probably in a populated area. If Pilgrennon is on Lewis, he will be well concealed and most likely isolated. It will be difficult to approach him undetected." She divided the food between two plates and placed one before Dana.

The police are still looking for missing school girl Dana Provine. Dana and Jananin both looked at the television.

Dana went missing from Coventry General Hospital on Wednesday night. Her foster parents are appealing to anyone who thinks they may have seen Dana to come forward.

The picture changed to an unrealistic image of a woman with sinister eyes and Jananin's hairstyle. Jananin's fork hit the table with a clang.

Police also want to question this woman, who was seen with a child matching Dana's description at a Bed and Breakfast in Staffordshire yesterday. She was seen driving a silver hatchback.

Jananin stared at the television. "I certainly cannot go to Lewis now."

"That doesn't look like you!" Dana protested.

Jananin turned back to Dana with a dry laugh. "If it doesn't look like me, how do you know it *is* me?"

This puzzled Dana.

"It's a police e-fit. They never look the same as who they are meant to be, but they have key features of that person's face people are supposed to be able to recognise."

"What does it mean, the police want to question you?"

"It means the evidence they have is only circumstantial."

"And what does that mean?"

"That they can't prove it was me who took you away. They can't even prove that it was me in Staffordshire, or you for that matter."

"Then they don't know it was you."

"Yes, but if they find me, they will find more evidence. Abducting a child is a serious charge. You say you don't like going to school. Prison is where the people who never matured enough to stop behaving like children in school end up."

Dana imagined a place of walls, full of Abigails. "Then you'll have to take me back to Graeme and Pauline's house."

Jananin met Dana's eyes with a fierce glare. "They have seen what he did to you. If you go back and they start doing more scans, more tests, it won't take them long to connect it with your abilities. Believe me, if the medical community finds out about you, Pilgrennon will as well. Whether he will want to capture you or kill you lest you be used against him at that point I can't say, but if people find out what you can do and why you can do it, you will have both him and the medical authorities of the world to contend with. Not to mention the risk that others will try to repeat or continue his experiments with whatever autistic children they can get their hands on."

Dana looked down at her half-eaten dinner. She no longer felt hungry.

"Come with me."

Jananin led Dana into the downstairs study opposite the living room. She pulled open the desk drawer. It was filled with glass bottles and jars.

"I had hoped I would not have to lay this burden on you." She placed a cylindrical glass tube with a metal screw cap in Dana's hand. "Dana, you must listen to me carefully now. You must not get this stuff on your skin. You must never, *ever* put it anywhere near your mouth."

"What is it?" Dana studied the white, salt-like substance in the vial.

"Its name is potassium cyanide. There is sufficient here to kill three men, but we only need to kill one. You must poison Pilgrennon with it. It will dissolve in water, but you must not put it into anything acidic — like anything that has vinegar or fruit juice in it — or it might make a vapour that will kill anyone near it."

"But how do I find Pilgrennon and put this in his food without him seeing me, especially if he's hiding on Lewis?"

"You're going to have to do what Pilgrennon expects you to do: go to him."

"But you said he would kill me!"

"I said he might try to kill you if he thought you were roaming the countryside and liable to expose him. He might kill you if he were to find out you were with me.

He won't hurt you if he thinks he can control you. That's the whole point of his beacon."

Dana looked at the glass vial in her hand, then back at Jananin. "Kill him? It's illegal to kill someone! They make you go to a prison for all your life!"

"You're a minor. You're not culpable. The law can argue that I gave you the means and I made you do it, but that's only if they catch you and you tell them I did. You can't be punished for a serious crime at your age."

"And what if they do that to you?"

"Yes, well, that will not happen to me, because I shall be staying here, and they will not have any evidence of my involvement. Pilgrennon is probably isolated. If you kill him, it may be no-one will even know he is dead. It could be nobody is aware he is living wherever he is in the first place. The murder of an outlaw is of little consequence. If he is ever found, it's unlikely any evidence to connect you to it will remain by the time."

Dana hesitated, staring at the vial. She tried to imagine herself putting this salty stuff in a glass of water, and the James Bond baddy at the crescent-shaped desk with the red button marked 'Compton Bomb' drinking it and falling off his swivel chair. "Why not just tell the police about Pilgrennon?"

Jananin let out a cold laugh. "I've already told the police about Pilgrennon. Little good it did, since he destroyed all the evidence there was at the time, and little good it would do bringing further evidence, particularly when the evidence concerned is *you*." Jananin looked at Dana in a way that made her feel uncomfortable.

"Oh, Pilgrennon would go to jail, but probably not for very long. You would be dragged through hospitals to be tested and experimented on, until they completely ruined your life and any semblance of normality, and they'd all declare how unethical it is and how deplorable that it happened here in the UK, and they'd pass laws to stop it ever happening again here, or in Europe, or the

USA. But think what some countries, where the rights of the individual do not matter, might do, in the light of this evidence, for the next biggest technological weapon."

Jananin closed the drawer with a conclusive force and stood up.

"You must do this, Dana. It is the only way. When Pilgrennon is dead, that beacon that disturbs your mind will be silenced forever. You will be able to go back to your home with your foster parents and live in freedom, and never have to worry about the device or the reason for it being discovered, or an unheralded blast of Compton radiation one day finishing you."

Dana didn't reply. She wondered if normal children, who weren't autistic and had proper families, went out hunting villains with their mothers. She supposed even people who broke the law must have families, so maybe this was how they start out on their careers as criminals, with a parent as a mentor. Perhaps being sent on poisoning errands for family members was seen as normal among some. Perhaps that was why social services took some children away from their families by force, as Graeme had implied, because parents were training children up as assassins.

Did it even count as a crime if it involved another criminal, who had done something wrong that the police had failed to act on? Did it make it different if someone was dangerous, as Jananin had explained to her this murderous experimenting thief Pilgrennon was? Dana had never known what it was to have a real parent, or what was usual to expect from such a relationship.

At least it wasn't school.

After several minutes, Jananin said, "Now, when is the next ferry to Stornoway?"

"Tomorrow." Dana closed her fingers over the vial in her hand, "9:30."

DANA watched Jananin's car drive off into a rainy predawn. The woman's eyes regarded her in the rear-view mirror before the car pulled onto the road and accelerated out of Dana's life. The car's brake lights flashed briefly as it dipped below the incline of the road.

Standing alone there, it was as though the lady who was really Dana's mother had never known she existed. She had driven away as would a stranger, or a social worker, or a failed foster placement, or any of the other types of people Dana came into contact with who made all the decisions about her life.

With Jananin went any aspirations of normality, and Dana suddenly wanted to know Jananin like a real daughter would know her mother, however that was, and not as a cold acquaintance; she wanted Jananin to come back and love her like a mother was meant to.

The lamps on the ferry terminal shone yellowy in the gloom. Behind, the lights of Ullapool glimmered at the base of the dark, rearing land.

How was she supposed to go to Lewis and find and poison a man she didn't even know, alone? She was stranded here in the outer reaches of civilisation, and Pilgrennon was sitting on Lewis somewhere, being evil and stroking his James Bond cat, the finger of his other hand hovering over the ignition of his Compton bomb.

But being alone was not Dana's problem. Other people were her problem. Other people didn't like Dana, and Dana didn't like them. Being alone meant being away from people like Abigail who wanted to hurt her. Being with other people was what made her panic, like she had in Miss Robinson's classroom when she'd broken the wLAN.

Shivering, Dana pulled her fur-trimmed hood up against the rain and sat behind the semicircular wall that bordered the parking area. Heathers grew from the edges of the concrete. She hugged the backpack Jananin had given her, which contained a laptop, clothes and food, and the cyanide vial, and concentrated on the reassuring pulse of the computer's WiFi on standby. Down here, sheltered from the wind with her eyes closed, it was just her and the computer. The nauseating open ocean and the ferry terminal and all the mountains and heather and dark cold emptiness might not be there. She might be sitting on the sofa in Pauline and Graeme's warm living room, the WiFi pulse from Graeme's laptop left on the coffee table.

A sound of tyres on the road roused Dana. She slowly raised her head so her eyes were just above the stone wall.

A saloon car with racing green paint pulled up. A man got out, pulling on his jacket and grimacing against the wind. After lighting a cigarette and looking at his watch, he stood staring out to sea, jiggling up and down with smoke flying in great streams over his shoulder.

After a few minutes he pointed something at the car, and Dana sensed a signal and heard it lock. He walked through flurries of rain the wind blew in from the sea towards a building marked 'Ullapool Ferry Terminal'.

Dana waited until he was out of sight before approaching the car. She concentrated on the blinking light on its dashboard.

The car unlocked.

The memory of Graeme on the television returned. Pauline and Graeme would be unhappy with her if they found out what she'd been doing. Perhaps she should look for a police station instead, and tell the police what Jananin had told her about Pilgrennon, and then they would take her back to Pauline and Graeme's house. She could go to the ferry terminal where the man had, say she was lost, ask for someone to take her to the police station.

But then she would have to go back to the school, and the hospital. Jananin had said Pilgrennon might hurt her in the future, and if he found out Dana had told the police about him, he might use a Compton bomb, and she wouldn't even know it was coming. And Jananin had told her: Pilgrennon had to be stopped before he did something else. Only Dana knew where the beacon was, and only she could go to Pilgrennon's hiding place without him becoming suspicious and setting off a Compton bomb.

Dana went to the back of the car and pressed the lock on the boot. It lifted. A golf bag and a holdall lay inside. She was relieved to notice as she climbed in that the boot door had a handle to open it from inside. She bent her knees slightly to fit in and pulled the boot door shut.

She told the car to lock from inside the boot. The man's bag smelt of aftershave and it made Dana sneeze. She pulled the sleeping bag Jananin had given her out of the backpack a little and tried to breathe through that. Dampness from the rain that had settled on Dana's clothing soon began to fill the warming atmosphere enclosed in the boot.

Soon, she heard cars pull up close to where she hid, their engines switching off.

The car wobbled in the wind. A great horn sounded, deep and distant. Dana stayed still and silent.

The central locking clicked, and she heard the front door open. She felt the jerk in the suspension as the man got in. The exhaust vibrated somewhere below her. The car began to move, towards the low concrete building beside the gate, where the road led to nothing but sea. Gravity's pull shifted and Dana and the golf bag rolled against the rear seats as the car tilted forward down the slope. Stones bounced off the underside of the chassis.

The golf clubs rattled behind her head. She hoped the man wasn't a lunatic who would drive the car into the sea.

The car slowed. Dana fidgeted in the confined space available to her. She could sense a security camera. The signal didn't penetrate the boot well, and all she could picture from it was the blurred outline of the car amongst a static snow. The front wheels rose and the car pivoted on its back axle. The engine pitch increased and the car lifted itself onto a smoother surface. Down it went again with a jolt. The engine switched off. Dana felt the man get out again. She curled up tightly, hoping he would not decide to get something from the boot. She counted twenty pulses from Jananin's computer.

The dull throb from without the car intensified. They must be moving, although she did not feel any sensation of acceleration. She had made it on to the ferry without being caught.

Dana could detect no cameras or mobile phones, and could hear no people moving outside the car. The air inside the boot had become very moist and unpleasant. The horrible alcoholic smell of the man's aftershave went right into her lungs with every breath. She pulled on the handle until the boot door popped up. Cautiously and very slowly, she slid over the lip of the boot to crouch between the bumpers. The cars were parked in two lines along white-painted walls on either side of the room. It looked like a subway, lit by electric lights. She saw no-one.

Dana shrugged her pack onto her shoulders and closed the boot door. She made her way between the cars to a doorway beyond which stairs led up. She read the words *Tier 2* painted on the wall, and looked back at the car to fix its position in her mind.

The stairs led up to a carpeted landing. She could feel the tremor of the ship's engine through the soles of her boots, and outside the windows stretched the grey surface of the ocean.

The enticing aroma of coffee led her down the corridor to a restaurant. It had been four hours since Dana had last eaten, but already she was hungry.

A very slight, unearthly sense of motion and imbalance could be detected through the floor. Dana reached the end of the food queue and nearly lost her balance, attracting the attention of the woman at the end. Dana fumbled in her skirt pocket where she'd put the handful of pound coins and roll of notes Jananin had given her. She peered furtively at the man serving the food up ahead.

As the queue slowly progressed, Dana noticed a man and woman standing in the corridor behind. The woman was bent over, making a face. "Shut up, Alasdair!" she said to the man.

"Perhaps you oughtn't to have eaten this morning," Alasdair said.

The woman put her hand over her mouth and made a doubled-over dash into the ladies' toilet. A few seconds later, Dana heard her vomiting in there, amplified in the bowl of a lavatory like an amphitheatre.

The man serving looked over the counter at her. He and the woman in front whom Dana had nearly fallen on exchanged a glance, and then the woman spoke to Dana, not unkindly. "Where's your mum and dad?"

The serving man smiled at her, but an anxious knot formed in Dana's stomach. She pointed back towards the corridor. "My mum went to the toilet to be sick. Can I have some lasagne please? I've got the money for it." She held out a handful of pound coins.

The man and woman made another exchange. The man gave her an understanding nod and shovelled steaming lasagne onto a plate. Dana paid for the meal and headed over to a table by the window. She looked down into the sea as she ate. The foam the boat threw up at its base was pure white froth, but staring into it revealed deep turquoise colours. Gulls flitted over the surface, occasionally diving into the water. Dana never saw one resurface. Perhaps they couldn't swim, like her. It was stupid of them to go into the water if that was so.

After she'd eaten and put her tray and dirty plate with the others, Dana found an observation lounge high up on the ship, with sofas clustered into the corners. From the front of the boat, she could see nothing, but she could sense Pilgrennon's beacon almost directly ahead, a singing, throbbing texture of rupturing orange.

The rain dwindled, leaving the sky an inscrutable grey. The light of the morning sun made a watery circle behind colourless clouds. Black rocks showed in the water, the sea flinging spray high into the air as though trying to reject the stuff of hard land. Even the swaying of the boat, gradually becoming stronger, suggested otherworldliness. It seemed this place was so remote even gravity didn't work right.

A man sat on an opposite sofa and opened a newspaper. Dana realised it was the same man whose car she had hidden in. It struck her as funny that he should sit opposite her and ignore her.

A pale shadow became visible on the water's horizon. It looked like a mountain had risen from the sea. Dana turned her head left and right, up and down, trying to pinpoint the source of Pilgrennon's beacon, but the only result she got was from the man, who lowered his newspaper and stared at her.

As the boat drew closer, the shape began to look more like a piece of land than a thicker clump of mist. Then an outflung limb of rock showed, passing the ship on the right-hand side: a stale cake with mouldy-green icing.

The boat headed for a cluster of lights trapped in a deep crack where the land let in the ocean. The island made Dana shudder. She could see no trees and very few houses. The houses she could see looked tiny and cold, like limpets clinging to bare rock at low tide, thin smoke rising from their chimneys. The land was a featureless blend of green and russet strewn with white boulders.

Dana picked up her bag and made her way back down to the cars. Certain no-one was looking, she opened the boot of the man's car and climbed back in.

Not long after, she felt the man get in. The louder engine quietened. All around, car engines started. The car moved forward and upwards, over the smooth surface, and down. It stopped briefly, then continued forwards. The car accelerated and changed gear. It felt like they were driving on a normal road now. Dana lost track of the number of turns they made. GPS was indistinct from here.

Finally, the car stopped. The suspension creaked as the man got out. She feared very much that he would open the boot this time, but he simply locked the car, and the scrunch of his feet on gravel receded.

Dana lay completely still and listened for several minutes. She couldn't sense any of the signals mobile phones gave off, but of course there could be plenty of people who did not have mobile phones, had forgotten them, or had flat batteries. The man could be smoking not far from the car.

She grasped the handle and pulled until the locking mechanism clicked. The boot door slowly rose. She saw more parked cars under an overcast sky, but no people. Dana swung her stiff legs over the edge of the boot and slid out. She picked up her bag and closed the boot door as quietly as she could.

The man had parked by a pub and was presumably in it. Ocean stretched away over the rise of the land, as it had at Ullapool, but GPS told Dana she was on Lewis and looking back east to the mainland.

She turned back to face west. Blurry oranges and pinks flickered over her vision. A faint sibilance stirred in her ears and a metallic taste filled her mouth.

Dana exited the car park found herself in a street below. She crouched behind a small hatchback car with grey paint. A wall hid her and the car from the pub. She saw no-one on the pavement or road.

Perhaps she ought to try to find a bus. Dana didn't know where to catch a bus, and she didn't know where to tell its driver she needed to go.

This was *wrong*, she thought as she looked through the window at the silver insignia on the steering wheel. She didn't have a driving licence. She wasn't allowed to drive; she was too young. Taking things that aren't yours is illegal. But then, driving too fast and talking on a mobile phone were illegal, and carrying a knife and having a sword in the boot were illegal, but Jananin had done them and the police hadn't found out.

Dana told the car to unlock and got in on the driver's side. She dumped her bag in the passenger's seat and put the seatbelt on. Rummaging through the glove compartment, she found a pair of sunglasses. She pulled down the mirror on the windscreen and scruffed her hair forward to obscure her face. She put on the glasses and pulled up the furry collar on her coat. From a distance, she hoped she might look like a young woman rather than a girl. Breathing rapidly, she studied the controls, trying to suppress the fear she had of the owner of the car suddenly appearing.

The gear lever had a diagram depicting different positions labelled with letters on the top of the knob. Dana tried to move it, but it was stuck. Perhaps the car had to be running before it would work. She pulled the lever under the seat and shuffled it forward as far as it would go, until her feet could reach the pedals. Which pedal did what? Why had she not looked when Pauline and Graeme and Jananin had driven with her in the front seat? Moreover, she seemed to recall those cars had three pedals in them and the gear lever had numbers on, instead of letters. The information she wanted would be on the Internet. She needed a wLAN now, but she could find none.

It couldn't be that hard. Dana remembered when Graeme had let her sit in his car and pretend to drive, standing on the pedals with her feet and pushing all the buttons and stalks on the dashboard to see what they did.

One of the pedals, Dana decided, must be a brake. Yes, when adults drove, they always trod on something to slow down and stop. She put both feet to the pedals. The right one went down without effect, but she felt resistance against the left. That one must be the brake.

She looked behind the car. Here was a problem: the road downhill went east. She needed to go west; uphill. In order to do this, she was going to have to get the engine to start. What did people use to start the car? The key, she supposed, or was that just for opening the doors? No, Graeme's cartoon key fobs used to knock against the dashboard in his car. So where did the key go? Dana felt around the steering wheel and found the keyhole on the right side.

Dana concentrated on the car's computer for a minute. The key had a code written on it in magnetic words. The car had to be able to read the code and there had to be something that conducted electricity in the keyhole next to the steering wheel, but the magnetic words didn't necessarily have to be written on the key. She could tell them to the computer through the IR for the central locking.

She put her hands in her skirt pocket and found the three fuses, but in the fluff and grit close to the seam, she felt the outline of a paperclip. She partly untwisted it and bit the end so it was bent to about the width the real key would be. She told the code to the car while she scratched about inside the hole with the paperclip.

Something caught inside the mechanism. The dials on the dashboard lit up and the engine whirred to life.

When she tried the gear lever again, it moved. It had started in *P*, and she had a choice of *R*, *D*, or *N*. Probably *R* was for reverse. She tried *N*.

Nothing happened. Dana took her foot off the brake. She trod on the right pedal. The engine roared loudly and she at once removed her foot. Heat spread across her face. At any moment, the car's owner could run into view and want to know why someone who couldn't drive was trying to steal his or her car.

She tried to move the gear lever to D, half expecting the car to make some other horrible noise, but it didn't. The gear lever was stuck. It took her a moment to work out that she had to put her foot on the brake to unlock it. Triumphantly, Dana put the car into D and took her foot off the left pedal. The car began to creep forward, and she hurriedly trod it down again to stop it going into the back of the car parked in front.

She carefully eased off the brake and turned the steering wheel. The car began to move into the road. Dana pressed the right pedal to make it go faster, but it creaked, and a judder ran through the chassis. An alarm sounded and a red light came up on the dashboard. She cringed at the noise the engine made, sure it would bring half the inhabitants of Stornoway running into the street.

There was another brake as well, she remembered, behind the gear lever, which Graeme had given her the one condition that she must not play with. She had seen that work from the back of cars; you had to press a button and push it down to release it. She did so. The car jerked forward and the warning light on the dashboard went off.

Over the summit of the hill, light showed in the windows of a bank and a pharmacist. A man in a dark green hooded coat walked on the pavement. The car began to gather speed. The needle on the hemispherical clock above the wheel began to rise towards 10 mph and the car steadily overtook the man on the pavement. Dana looked the other way as she passed him. She turned the steering wheel to follow the road right, but not fast enough. The left tyres trundled over grass and the car wandered across the other side of the road before she managed to get it back on the left.

Pilgrennon's beacon came from the west now. GPS showed Dana the way to the A858. Cars tore past on her right, blaring their horns. She trod on the right pedal until the needle on the speed dial rose to 30 mph, keeping close to the left side of the road. The car felt unstable and the wind roared past. She gripped the steering wheel hard.

The road crossed a barren landscape, devoid of anything larger than tiny, isolated cottages. A left turn approached opposite a concrete shelter-thing, leading in the direction she sensed the beacon. She trod on the left pedal hard and the deceleration threw her forward, digging the seatbelt into her chest. Fighting the steering wheel, she turned the car into the smaller road. Stony cliffs rose on either side, miniature waterfalls pouring down the sides to feed streams running alongside the road. Sheep ate coarse grass on the verges and stood in the way, not moving aside until she drove up close. A mist descended upon the land as she steered along the winding road.

Pilgrennon's beacon shifted as she continued, moving north. She must be near now. The road turned sharply right. The car sensed it was getting dark and turned its headlamps on unprompted. Catseyes glimmered under a veil of fog. Closer. The susurration in her ears became a whisper of encouragement, *closer, closer…*

The road bore left, and now the beacon was almost due north. The whispering in Dana's right ear increased in pitch, becoming a desperate plea for her not to leave. She turned her head towards the sound. Shapes moved in the fog like veiled dancers.

The surface under the left front tyre changed abruptly. A thick post loomed an instant before impact. A clang of metal and a bang like something exploding. Dana's vision turned white. Something walloped her in the face, flinging her back against the driver's chair.

The car was full of smoke, and at first she thought it was fog from outside, until she smelled burning. She fumbled for the handle and threw the door open. Cold fog mingled with the smoke in the car.

The centre of the steering wheel had blown apart and white fabric was hanging out. Dana stared at it. Was it part of the engine? No, it was an airbag, she remembered. They blew up to stop people hitting their heads in a crash.

She undid her seatbelt and dragged the bag out of the car. The front of the car between the headlamps had been smashed in by a post holding up a sign reading *Timsgearraidh ½, Aird Uig 1*. Dana stared at the hulk of the car shrouded in the cold fog. Whoever owned it was not going to be happy.

She looked back to the north as she pulled the straps of her pack onto her shoulders. She may as well follow the signal rather than rely on the road. From what Jananin had said, Pilgrennon was not likely to be near a road at any rate.

Wrapping her arms around herself against the chill, damp mist, she stumbled over ground that here was just stones and grass and puddles. She glanced back at the car, its door open and internal light still on. In the mist, the light took on a ghostly, unreal quality.

Daylight began to fade. The cliffs closed ranks, blocking her route, and she came upon road again, a single track of broken concrete, grass growing in its crevices. She walked beside it in case any traffic came, but none did.

The road rose sharply. She passed a dilapidated house on the hill, the glow of electric lights colouring a few of its windows. A ditch covered with bars perpendicular to the road interrupted her path. To stop animals from entering. Wire fencing stretched away on either side. She trod carefully over the rusty bars and continued along the road.

A square, flat-roofed building loomed in the fog. As she approached, it became apparent the concrete was falling away, revealing rubble and rusty metal rods, the windows empty of glass and covered only by planks of wood battered by the elements. She followed the road as it turned. More buildings, similarly deserted. What was this place? GPS wouldn't tell her. The road was unnumbered; perhaps this place of ruined houses was too small to be listed on the map.

Was Pilgrennon here? The signal was close now. Dana began to run along the road, compelled by some deep instinct. The air smelt of the sea, and the cold and the dying light no longer bothered her. She passed the last of the abandoned buildings and kept running, jumping another metal grid in the road. The road sloped uphill. Through the fog, she made out of a tall fence crowned with barbed wire. She ran over the stony ground as the road swept away and threw herself against the gate, trying to discern what lay behind it.

"Hello?"

Her shout came weak and empty in the fog. She took her hands away from the mesh, breathing slowing. A padlock hung from the gate, and in the dimming light she could only just read the sign fixed to the wire:

MINISTRY OF DEFENCE
This is a prohibited place within the meaning of the Official Secrets Act.
Unauthorised persons entering this area may be arrested and prosecuted.

The boxy shapes of more concrete buildings were visible in the fog behind the fence. Pilgrennon's beacon was no longer ahead, but to her left, the west. She stepped away from the fence, off the road. The ground squelched and her boots sank into a rivulet of dark water saturating the black soil beside the road. The water ran over the surface ahead, down an incline hidden by fog and fading daylight. The wind roared and tore at her hair. Either GPS or some instinct common to all living things told her she was nearing a cliff. The pounding of the waves sounded very close.

She stared into the mist that shimmered and rippled at the point of her focus. A kaleidoscope of colours spiked from the point of the invisible beacon. *You are close, you are close. Come, come.*

A faint light pulsed and disappeared.

Dana blinked. A few seconds later, the light came again, and again, a rhythmic rising and fading and rising and fading every thirty seconds or so. Dana closed her eyes. The spectral lines coming from the beacon remained, even though she could not possibly be seeing them in reality. The pulsing light did not return. She waited thirty more seconds, then opened her eyes. The light came again. She concentrated, blocking out the signal momentarily. There was a real, pulsing light out there in the mist, at the same position as the beacon. She checked GPS. This was the end of the land. There was nothing out there but ocean, and then Greenland. Cold bit through the fur lining of Dana's coat. Her feet had gone numb inside her boots.

Pilgrennon's beacon was not on Lewis. It was inside a light, in the sea.

–8–

DANA stumbled back down the road, bent against the wind, into the doorless rectangular arch of a small concrete building. Rusted hulks of old machinery scattered the floor inside, hardly visible in the fading dusk that penetrated the boarded-up shell.

Rubble and broken glass crunched under her feet. Breathing hard, she slid the backpack off her shoulders to the floor. She pulled the computer out and squatted down with it balanced on her knee.

There was an icon in the middle of the screen labelled 'phoneclient'. Dana ran the program. A database appeared with a list. Most of the entries were people's names, but 'Aberdeen-house' not far from the top caught her attention. She selected it.

Through the feeble speakers of the computer came a tinny rendition of a phone ringing.

"Hello?"

"Jananin!"

"Dana?"

"Jananin, Pilgrennon's beacon isn't on Lewis; it's in the sea." The gravity of where she was and what she had done at once overwhelmed Dana, and her explanation came out in a sob.

"Dana, I can't understand you! Where are you? Speak clearly!"

"Jananin, I can't do this any more! I'm scared! I need you to come and get me."

"Pull yourself together!" The indignance in Jananin's voice wasn't lost over the crackling telephone transmission. "Of *course* you can do it! Now where are you?"

"I'm on the west coast of Lewis, and Pilgrennon's beacon is still wester than this. There's only sea in front of me, and there's a light that keeps flashing where the beacon is."

"A flashing light? Is it a lighthouse? A kind of beacon built on a rock in the sea, to show ships not to run into the rocks. Can you give me coordinates?"

"Coordinates? I don't know what coordinates are!"

"They're the numbers you get from GPS that tell you where you are."

"I don't know any numbers from GPS! I just imagine a map and GPS tells me where I am on it!"

"Look, when my SatNav, or any computer, reads GPS, it triangulates its position using a sequence of numbers from satellites — coordinates — that tells it where it is, and it translates these numbers via a program to a location on a map. The number will be in the machine code, not in the program with the map."

Dana tried to work out what Jananin meant and how it translated to what she understood of GPS, but it made no sense. "I don't understand."

"Can you tell me what the nearest place is called that you do know the name of? Are there any unusual features about the landscape where you are now?"

"There's a fence that says I can't go in. There are some houses, but they're old and no-one lives in them. I don't know what it's called. I think it's too small to go on the map. I went up a road — I think it was the B8011."

There came a long pause. Dana heard Jananin rifling through the pages of a road map on the other end of the telephone. "That doesn't narrow it down a lot."

"What am I going to do? It's getting dark and there's no-one here!."

"Dana, you've done well to get this far. I think it's probably best if you find somewhere you can sleep until tomorrow morning. You said there were some uninhabited houses. Do any of them have roofs?"

"I think so," said Dana.

"Why don't you go and have a look at them and see if there's one you can sleep in?"

Dana didn't exactly feel optimistic about this suggestion, but Jananin's tone of voice had calmed down, and this had gone some way to quell her own panic.

"I'll get on the ferry to Lewis as soon as I can and work out where you are, but it's likely not going to be possible until tomorrow afternoon. Stay in your current location and avoid people. You'll feel better after you've slept. If you feel worried again, you can always call me on the computer."

"Jananin?" But Jananin had hung up.

Dana stepped back out into the wind. The moon had risen and the fog had mostly cleared. Dana held her head up bravely to the stars, marvelling at the number in the darkness here. They formed a misty band across the sky at their densest point. If Jananin wouldn't be afraid, Dana told herself, then she wouldn't be afraid.

Sheep looked up at her in the silver moonlight as she tramped across the waterlogged moor. They ran away when she got close. Dana forced a weak laugh. The sheep weren't scared of this place, and if sheep were scared of Dana but not scared of here, then the laws of algebra said that Dana shouldn't be scared of here either, because Dana>sheep>here. She wasn't alone, with the sheep and the computer and Pilgrennon's beacon to keep her company.

She thought again of how Abigail and her henchgirls had made her feel, when she was walking back to Pauline and Graeme's, and when they trapped her in the toilet. Abigail meant to hurt her, so she had good reason to be scared of her. This place wouldn't hurt her just because it was cold and dark and unfamiliar. Other people were Dana's problem, not aloneness. In this way she could make herself think of it differently: a good place, away from bad people.

Most of the boxy concrete houses were boarded up, but Dana found one with a blank hole where the window had been, and climbed through it without much trouble. Dust and small rubble covered the floor, but it was dry and didn't smell. She got into the sleeping bag Jananin had given her and settled the bag with the computer in under her head like a pillow.

Dana woke some time before dawn. The floor was cold and the bits on it dug into her. When she felt her way to the paneless square window through which she'd forced her way, she saw nothing but stars and the featureless dark land.

Pilgrennon's beacon drummed in her head. A telephone mast back down the road somewhere had started to annoy her, and together they were a pair of out-of-synch musicians. She lay for an hour trying to sleep, but the noise in her thoughts and the cold kept her awake.

She took Jananin's computer out and turned it on. The screen was blinding in the darkness.

She found many, many files in a folder called *Pilgrennon*. She opened the first graphics file. It showed a photograph of a building made of glass and metal, with a bridge connecting the first floor to another similar building. The buildings stood on a gently undulating lawn around which stone paths wound. Little patches of spring flowers and many trees with white flowers but no leaves grew around the paths and near the bridge.

The next picture showed the same buildings, but the side of the nearest building had been ripped out in what looked like an explosion, shattering the glass on the bridge. The grass had been turned to mud by vehicle tyres, and the flowers had fallen off the trees, trampled into a pinkish-brown mulch by hundreds of feet. A thin blue-and-white striped ribbon bisected one corner of the picture.

Dana opened an HTML file. It was a page from an

online newspaper.

Dr Ivor Pilgrennon is wanted for questioning on the ethics of his scientific practice regarding the work he has been conducting at the Institute of Neurodivergence in Oxford. The Institute, which is mostly owned by Dr Pilgrennon's company, was this morning damaged by an explosion, the cause of which is yet to be ascertained. No persons have been injured.

The article was small, without even a picture. There were several other articles on the page, about council houses and education.

Dana shut down the computer. The cracks in the concrete walls were becoming visible. Outside, the mountainous bulk of Lewis had become visible against a salmon east horizon. The sun rose behind a curtain of mist as she ate the cheese and biscuits Jananin had given her and drank water from her flask.

Coloured lichens broke off the concrete under her hands as she climbed through the window. She saw no trees or vegetation other than the short grass, whose blades trembled constantly in the stiff wind that blew out to sea. Pools of water rippled on the sodden ground. This empty landscape had few features, just the concrete houses, the single-track road, and the distant fence, which Dana could now see surrounded more derelict buildings, larger than the others, and tall white masts. The land terminated sharply behind the fence.

The wind rose as she headed along the road, making for the house she had seen the light behind the windows the night previous, part of a small group of stony cottages clinging to the rock and grass, exposed to the wind and standing against the oblivion of the grey sky.

A rusty old car stood in the road. Only the one stone cottage, whose windows had been lit the night before, looked as though anyone lived in it. The others stood with crumbling walls and smashed windows, the slates that made up their roofs a mess of angles and gaps.

With a start, she noticed an old man sitting on the concrete steps of the one inhabited house. Had he been there all the time she had been looking at the houses? His head bowed forward, hat tipped over his face.

The man cleared his throat with a whirring cough, making her start. "Ye're not from round here, are ye, lass?"

"No," Dana nervously replied. She hoped he hadn't been watching the news recently. He didn't look like the sort of man who had a television. If he did have one, perhaps he might not sit in his garden, if it could be called a garden. It looked like a rockery with no plants, apart from an ivy growing up the wall of the house.

"Ye're mum and dad come here for Hogmanay?"

Dana watched the man. "I don't know."

"What do yere mum and dad do?"

Dana hesitated. "My mum is a scientist." She paused again and thought of Graeme. "My dad works in an office."

The man raised his eyebrows. They disappeared under the brim of his hat.

She turned to look out to sea. "What's that light?"

"That's the Flannans."

Dana looked back at him over her shoulder. "The what?"

"The Flannans. The Flannan Isles. And their haunted lighthouse."

"Haunted?" The light flashed again.

"Aye. In the winter of 1900, the three lighthouse keepers vanished, ne'er to be seen again."

The wind blew Dana's hair away from her face as she stared at the pulsing light. "Does a ferry go there?"

"No. No-one goes there. The island looks like a claw." The man lifted his head, eyes widening under the brim of the hat. He held out his hand, crooked fingers bent down into a grasping pose.

Spokes of colour radiated from the lighthouse. Dana

sensed a deep thrum, like a tuning fork, just beyond the limits of her hearing. If that was where Pilgrennon was…

"Were the lighthouse keepers murdered?"

"Nobody knows. Maybe they were. By *something*."

Dana started to walk down the road in the direction she'd come the night before.

"It's only a story, lass!" the old man shouted after her. "I wouldn'a worry about it!"

There was no point following the road back inland. Dana retraced her steps down the steep road to the mouth of the stream. The rough outline of Lewis's coast that she had in her mind showed the land to the east breaking into coves, unlike the craggy headland that bent around to the north.

She picked her way across the stream, stepping on large boulders lying in the rushing water. The ground rose steeply, and Dana found little sheep-trails to scramble up. At the top of the incline the wind was very strong. She turned back towards Pilgrennon's beacon. The fog had cleared and the light no longer flashed. The concrete houses where she had spent the night clustered on the bleak hill before the masts behind the fence, and beyond the promontory she distinguished two faint shapes in the sea. One of them must be the island with the beacon on it.

The land fell again, and rose into a series of crags. A little farther inland she found a single track road. She followed it over the next hill and found herself looking down upon a pale beach and a clutch of stone houses edging the road. Most had sparse gardens and cars parked on their driveways.

On the beach stood a few shabby boats, some lying at 45-degree angles. Things on the masts jangled like bells in the wind. A few peculiar little cages made of rope, with funnels narrowing into either side, lay in a heap on the shore.

The houses came to an end a few yards on. GPS

suggested there might be a few more a little farther along. Beyond them, all she could see was empty heath and sky.

As she stood there, looking at the boats, a thought came to her. Jananin had told her to stay here and wait, but if she could catch a ferry, and she could drive a car, surely it could not be that difficult for her to drive a boat?

Dana looked to check no-one was watching. She headed for the smallest of the boats — a blue-painted one made of wooden planks, lying upside-down like the protective shell of a limpet. Dana got hold of the edge of the boat and heaved it up. It fell on one side of its keel, but fortunately the sand made little noise. A grubby white plastic case showed at the back of the boat. This must be where the engine was. It had a ring pull on it, which reminded her of one of those toys that make a noise. Perhaps boats worked the same way, and you had to pull a string to make them go.

She set her hands against the splintery back of the little boat and shoved it towards the sea. The side scraped on the ground. Dana dug the toes of her boots into the sand and locked her arms, pushing against the boat by straightening her legs. The boat slid. Once it was moving, it was easier to keep it moving.

The front of the boat slapped against the water. It lurched forward, righting itself. Dana hung on to the back corner of it. She stared at the boat in the water in trepidation. It didn't float steadily, wobbling with every wave. Dana held onto the side of it and tried to put her foot inside, but every time she put any weight there, the boat tilted and threatened to capsize. The waves ran in and out over her feet; her knees shook and her stomach felt like jelly. Finally, she put her foot as far into the boat as she could and threw herself over the side as quickly as possible. She landed with her feet sticking up. She twisted onto her knees and looked over the side. The momentum of getting in and the motion of the waves had caused the boat to drift farther from the shore. Water slopped under the keel. Dana crouched low in the boat against the alarming swaying. She stuffed her rucksack under the wooden plank that served as a seat, fearing water would come in and make the computer wet.

She'd have to go round the headland. The boat was pointing the right way. Dana grasped the ring on the engine, hanging on to the side of the boat with her other hand. She pulled at it and the cord jerked out and snapped back with a noise. The engine hadn't started. She was going to have to pull that cord *hard*.

She stood up, holding the side of the boat. The dark sea moved incessantly, the boat seeming perilously low in the water. *I'll fall, I'll fall...* She held the cord with both hands and put her feet against the board under the engine. It felt horribly unstable. In one violent motion, she leaned back and straightened her knees. She landed in the bottom of the boat, and the engine whirred and started up.

At first she couldn't work out why the boat wasn't moving, but then she found a lever on the white plastic box with four positions marked on it, like the gear lever in the car. It was in position 0, so she moved it to position 1. The pitch of the motor changed and the boat began to move away from the land.

Dana found a wooden handle under the engine. By trial and error, she worked out how to steer the boat. She guided it around the rocks, avoiding the dark shapes in the water where more rocks lurked beneath the surface. She moved the lever up to position 2, then 3, as she became more comfortable with the controls.

As she passed the headland where the masts and the concrete houses were, the shape of the two islands ahead became visible once more. She sat on the plank over the computer and listened to its pulse, apprehension at the approaching mass of rock rising in her.

Could Pilgrennon have murdered the lighthouse

keepers?

But the old man had said what — 1900. Dana thought of history lessons, more than 100 years ago, before computers, before Hitler and the Second World War and before even the First World War. Pilgrennon couldn't possibly have been alive in 1900, unless he was... well over 100. From what Jananin had said and from what she'd been able to work out from the overheard conversation between Mr Harris and Dr Osric, Pilgrennon had run away six months after Dana was born. He wouldn't have been here in 1900.

Birds flew over the boat, screeching. They had scaly red flippers for feet and ugly faces with beady white eyes. Dana hated them. She crouched low in the boat, concentrating on the computer's signal and trying to ignore the birds.

Every time she looked up, the lighthouse and the shifting coloured spokes and susurrating whisper of Pilgrennon's beacon were closer. At last she made out details on the rocks. The lighthouse stood, a white pillar, on the largest and closest, upon the rise of a high cliff.

Nearer to the island, Dana saw steps cut into the rock, winding treacherously up the heights, and a concrete place at the base for tying up boats.

Pilgrennon's beacon was not coming from the same island as had the lighthouse on it; it came from one of the other islands, a large one behind the lighthouse island, for there were several, some large with high cliffs and grass covering their peaks, but many barely more than protruding stones. As the boat passed the largest island, she saw the steps were badly weathered. She was glad she did not have to climb them. The island looked barren and empty, black rock standing out against a leaden sky. Dana shuddered where she crouched in the boat. It was easy to imagine it being haunted by the ghosts of dead lighthouse keepers.

She turned the boat as it approached the far island,

guiding it around as she sought a place to land.

As she passed the main outcrop, huge black pillars towered from the sea, the closest leaning to the land and forming a craggy arch, asymmetrical and ancient, horrible, like a ruined castle. The light was fading and a bank of approaching fog hung beyond the island like a saturated blanket. Behind her, the lighthouse began to cast its cold beam over the gleaming sea.

For the first time ever, the beacon was coming from the east. A thin mast of metal scaffolding reached high into the grey sky from the land ahead. *That was Pilgrennon's beacon!* But she could see no houses nearby. The rise of the cliff below the pillars had a stony shore at its base. She could land the boat there.

She secured the bag back on her shoulders and steered in. The cliff rose, swallowing the sky. Dana slowed the boat to position 1, and then 0, and let it slide closer to the shore on its momentum alone.

When stones grated under the keel, Dana jumped clear. Her foot splashed into the water, a slimy rock gave way, and her ankle twisted sideways. Cold water filled her boot. She fell forward on hands and knees in the shallows, her mouth filling with rank salty water.

The boat rasped along the gravel. Her foot must have caught the lever as she'd fallen out, because the engine pitch had changed. Dana was on her feet before she could think and wading after the boat, the freezing water coming up past her knees and gripping her legs against the will of her muscles. She lunged desperately, but already it was yards away in deep water.

Dana gasped at the cold that penetrated as sharply as a knife, at the sight of the boat heading out for Greenland by itself. She backed away from the dark water, towards the shore. The black rock of the cliff engulfed the sky. Dana clutched her arms around herself and shivered. The beacon was right above, blaring and thundering, filling her mouth with a peppery taste and her sight with weird colours.

Shaking, she dropped her backpack on the shore and pulled the computer out. It was a miracle it had not got wet and it still worked. She opened up its screen and ran the phone program to call Jananin's Aberdeen house.

A message came up on the screen. *No signal.*

A shuddering cry escaped Dana. She looked out to sea, where she could no longer see the boat, and then back at the towers of rock in the crashing swell upon the inhospitable shore. A fear like no fear she'd ever felt before closed in on her.

-9-

FOG was drifting in fast, the air becoming wet and thick. Dana began to make her way along this forbidding shore on knees weak from shock and the cold of the water.

Down among the black rocks, treacherous with slimy marine vegetation, the sickening rearing of the swell threatened to engulf her, appearing to heave taller than she stood. Every wave that struck the shore loosed a stench and set rocks and stones moving and settling upon one another in the backwash with an overwhelming *crack*.

Dana's nausea made the island of rock feel afloat and imperilled on the sea. She skidded on a rock, putting one foot into a freezing pool. A crab lurked unmoving, its claws and legs drawn in front of it like a Swiss army knife displaying its many blades. Small rubble came rattling down the cliff face, drawing her sight in search of its unseen cause to the stark rock against the sky. Desolation, dead and empty of computer stimuli, yet alive with the wrath of nature. GPS and Pilgrennon's hissing beacon above her head were all she could make sense of.

She could see no way up the cliff to the beacon. If it even *was* a beacon. What if it was just some communications mast that by coincidence particularly affected her senses? Jananin had never ascertained whether it was or wasn't a beacon. It was simply a signal Dana had been aware of and had assumed was the beacon Jananin spoke of. And Jananin had only assumed the existence of a beacon in the first place. It was an assumption grounded on an assumption. What if Pilgrennon wasn't here, had never been here, didn't want to be found?

Panic swelled inside her, restricting her breathing. Why had she come here? Why hadn't she waited like Jananin had told her? What if she was stuck here to die of cold, or of thirst or hunger? Or from being frightened. She could imagine what Pauline would say if she knew: *Dana what on Earth do you think you're doing? Stealing boats and cars and getting yourself stranded in the middle of nowhere because some stranger told you to.*

Daylight was fading fast. Each passing of the lighthouse's eerie beam Dana feared would illuminate things of a horribleness too great for her to imagine: monstrous black silhouettes upon the cliff against the sky, slimy tentacles reaching out from the sea and writhing over the rocks. She did not want to see this place in the dark!

She picked her way towards the pillars, the cliff becoming steeper with fewer stones to walk on so she had to cling to the wet rockface, aware she was whimpering with each breath. A shower of pebbles and earth fell past not far from her ear. Out in the sea, a greasy bird head surfaced on a curved neck looking too thin to support it, and sank again.

Waves pounded the bases of the contorted columns. Where the final pillar leaned in an arch against the island, a deep fissure had been eroded into the land. She felt inside it with her foot and found rock to stand on. The beam of the lighthouse swept by, casting a bedraggled shadow of herself on the rockface opposite. The sea roiled some twelve feet below.

She held the bag with Jananin's computer in it to herself tightly and stepped into the dark, her free hand held out in front of her, touching clammy rock with her fingers. The floor was not level, and Dana's sense of balance was made worse by the darkness and the uneven surface underfoot. She went into the cliff ten paces or so before her hand touched stone in front. She could see nothing of what lay within, only the crack of empty sky behind.

Dana's hand fell upon something flat: smooth and cold.

Metal.

She ran her hands frantically over the surface, searching for a handle. The surface was flat, rutted with flecks of rust from the salt spray, going as far up as she could reach, edges flush against rock.

No, there was a lock, a lock like the one on a car. On a car there was a red light where the signal for the lock came out. This didn't have a light.

Dana told the door to open.

For a second, nothing happened. Then a faint sound of machinery came alive. The door slid back into a recess in the rock. Behind it, a bulb with a cage around it cast a blue light upon the damp cavity.

She stepped through the doorway. Concrete stairs and a rusting steel handrail descended into cold Atlantic stone.

Something about that blue light brought the seawater taste back into Dana's mouth. The muscles in her sides tightened painfully. Bending double, she tried to stop herself from being sick, but it came anyway. She tried to breathe; tried to swallow; tried to do anything to stop retching. Dana put her hands over her ears and closed her eyes. At last she managed to inhale and cough.

She took her hands away from her head. She could no longer hear the noise of the sea, and GPS had disappeared like it did in Jananin's car. The door had closed behind her. She cautiously opened her eyes and stood upright.

"Signals can't come down here," she whispered to herself. Her own voice provided a little reassurance in the stillness. Experimentally, she tried to reopen the door, but it didn't work; the sensor was on the outside. What if she couldn't get back out? Not that being back out where she'd come from would help her any more than being in, with no boat and no way to call for help. There were lights on in here, so there must be people or computers inside.

Dana looked over the rail and down the stairs. Clutching her rucksack, she descended. A doorless rectangular entrance with a crack in the top of its concrete frame led off to the right. Inside, bright lamps in inverted metal boxes hung from the ceiling. The floor was sunk below the level of the entrance and covered with soil, and lines of plants with dark green, thickly veined leaves grew from it.

At the end of the corridor stood a doorway like that to the room with the plants. Voices and a clatter of objects drifted through. She looked back up the stairway. The way back was no longer open. The only way forward was what lay ahead. She stepped silently to the doorway and looked through discreetly.

The corridor opened into a large concrete room with cracked and stained walls. The black rock from which the island was made showed where the ceiling had fallen in. A large, irregular piece of concrete a few feet thick, lying in the centre of the room, was being used as a dining table by a man, a girl, and a boy wearing a helmet that came down over his eyebrows, riveted together down the middle and with blunt metal horns on either side. The plates and bowls they ate from were made of dented metal and plastic, and the cutlery was all bent and misshapen.

The boy looked up as he stuffed a potato into his mouth. He stared at Dana from under his helmet with his mouth open and the potato suspended from his upper teeth, until the man noticed him and followed his gaze to the doorway.

"Epsilon," said the girl. She was tall and thin with lank mousy hair. She did not even look at Dana, but stared directly ahead with a vacant countenance. Although there were no computers in the room, Dana sensed a signal. Not a computer signal. More like the signal she could feel from Cale when he was deeply asleep.

"Epsilon?" the man gasped, halfway through pushing back his seat and rising. His eyes were wide. The potato dropped from the boy's mouth and rolled onto the floor, but no-one paid it any heed.

The man stepped towards Dana. He held out his hand as though to a falcon he had lost, one that might fly away if startled. One of the stark bulbs on the wall revealed him to be a very tall, broad-shouldered, thickset man, with curly light-brown hair combed neatly from a centre parting and pressed flat. He wore metal-framed glasses halfway down his nose and a dark waistcoat, laced up at the front, over a crumpled checked shirt with the sleeves rolled up to the elbows. There were scratches and scabs on his forearms. Dana supposed from the slight lines at the edges of his eyes that he was in his early forties.

He stared at her, forehead creasing, mouth open. Dana was not good at working out what people's expressions meant, but for the length of time he looked, she guessed at disbelief, amazement, and unease.

Dana's sleeves and her legs up to her knees were wet, and she broke out in a convulsive shiver. "Good grief!" the man exclaimed. He went to the other side of the room to retrieve a blanket, which he flung around her shoulders.

"I'm sorry," said Dana. "I came here on a boat, and I fell out of it while I was trying to land it, and it kind of went without me."

The man was shaking his head. "Don't be sorry. There's nothing to be sorry for. Is there anybody else here with you?"

"No."

The man frowned. "Who was steering the boat?"

"Me."

He stared at her for what seemed a long time. "Come," he said, his voice shaky, "come, sit with us." He guided Dana by the shoulder to the place on the end of the table, between where he had sat and the boy. He scraped the metal chair he'd been sitting on towards her, the noise for a moment making Dana think she would be sick again. His hands shook as he set a plate, bowl, and mug before her. "What is your name?"

"Dana Provine." Dana's voice echoed unnervingly in the cold subterranean hall.

"Well, Dana," said the man as he poured water unsteadily into Dana's mug; the water was slightly brown. "Don't worry about that," he added. "It is clean — it's just discoloured from the filtering process." He spoke with a soft, deep voice. "It is very good to see you here. My name is Ivor Pilgrennon."

Dana thought she must have flinched or otherwise given herself away, even though she had suspected his identity.

Pilgrennon pulled up a folded chair lying against the wall. He unfolded it and sat on it. "This is Alpha." He motioned to the girl, who made no move to acknowledge either him or Dana. Her lank hair trailed over her shoulders and down her back, but was cut shorter at the front to hide her forehead, where Dana could discern a thick scar running vertically down to a point between her eyebrows. She wore a dress of sorts made from a scientist's lab coat over a jersey and pair of trousers of a dark grey material.

The boy in the helmet had been staring at Dana since she'd entered the room. He wore a similar dark jersey and trousers, underneath a waistcoat that appeared to have been patched together from the remains of numerous garments of varying colour. "This is Peter." Pilgrennon introduced him as he put two potatoes on Dana's plate.

Peter stuck his tongue out at Dana.

Pilgrennon asked, "Would you like some of this salad?"

Dana took some of the rubbery green strands she

was offered and put them on her plate, conscious of her wet clothes and the dirty smears on her hands. She drank some of the water, which didn't exactly taste like plain water, but quenched her thirst and rid her mouth of the taste of vomit and seawater. The old metal mug she'd been given was so bashed about it didn't stand evenly when she set it down. She stared at the steaming red things on the table that looked like a cross between wasps and crabs.

Pilgrennon said, "If you buy lobsters in a restaurant, they're quite expensive and they're considered something of a delicacy." Then he added, "I myself am personally sick of the sight of them, but they're probably interesting if you've not tried them before and you're hungry."

He picked up one of them and twisted the large pincers off it. He hit the body with a claw hammer several times, and Dana saw the surface of the concrete they were using as a table was scratched and chipped from this procedure. Pilgrennon put the lobster body on Dana's plate and started hitting one of the claws.

Dana pulled the head off the lobster. She found she could get most of the meat out of the body this way. It was like a prawn.

Pilgrennon gave one of the claws to Peter and the other to Alpha. "The things I'd give for a good steak and some chips." He smiled. "Eat your dinner, Alpha."

Alpha started to eat the lobster meat in a mechanical way. Peter had picked up the lobster's head and was sticking his fingers inside it, making faces at Dana as he did.

"Peter, don't be disgusting," said Pilgrennon. He picked up the other lobster and started pulling it apart.

Dana cautiously tried the green things, suspecting they might be seaweed as she chewed the gelatinous, rubbery texture. Peter took the lobster shell she had discarded and started cracking the legs with a pair of nutcrackers. He put one of the legs on Dana's plate.

Dana found her attention wandering to Pilgrennon's mug of water. She thought of the cyanide. The back of her neck crawled. Here and now, Jananin's request that she put the white salty substance in the tube in the bag under her chair in Pilgrennon's food had expanded to daunting proportions. She couldn't do that to this man, could she? He was sharing his dinner with her, not cackling or delivering a monologue about how he intended to use Compton bombs to take over the world.

She made furtive observations of Peter and Alpha. Jananin hadn't said anything about other children being here. Were they normal children, like Laura at the school? Were they horrible children, like Abigail? Or were they something else entirely: dangerous like Pilgrennon?

For a while, nobody spoke. The noise of cutlery and chewing sounded loud in the empty space. Dana looked up at the ceiling. Rusting iron poles poked from the gap the piece they were using as a table had fallen from.

"Where is Dana going to sleep?" said Peter.

Pilgrennon looked at Peter without moving his head, chewing, and shifted his eyes to look at Dana. "That depends whether Dana wants to stay here or not."

"I lost my boat," said Dana. "And the door doesn't open from inside."

Pilgrennon raised his eyebrows. "It doesn't open from either side. You need a mechanical key from the inside and either the same key or an electronic code from the outside." He stuck his bottom lip out in a strange sort of shrug, swallowed, and leaned his elbows on the table.

Dana ate her last potato and put her fork down. She looked down at the dirt on her hands. Was he playing games with her? Surely he had intended for her to open the doors. This man could not be trusted. He had stolen Jananin's gametes. Whatever gametes were. But could this really be the Pilgrennon Jananin Blake had described, who had caused Dana's birth to prove a theory and destroyed things with Compton bombs?

Pilgrennon wiped his mouth on a piece of cloth from his pocket. "Peter, can you clean this up please?" He stood up.

Peter began picking up the plates, his eyes fixed on Dana, but Alpha remained seated, staring ahead.

Pilgrennon stepped away from his chair and turned to face Dana. The odd eloquence in the way he moved his hands and the mobility of his facial expressions was somehow incongruous with his physical size. "I can open the door and take you back to Lewis, Dana, if that's what you'd like, but before I try to explain anything to you, I'm sure you would like a shower and some dry clothes."

He put his hand on Dana's shoulder and steered her towards a door at the opposite end of the hall to that by which she had entered, into a corridor much like the other one.

Inside another room with a damp, fungal odour, he handed Dana a towel from a shelf of misshapen slats built into an alcove. He found some clothing in another cupboard. "These used to be Alpha's, but they will probably fit you." "I have to go before Peter breaks a metal plate." Pilgrennon smiled briefly. He turned to disappear around the corner of the corridor.

The dull rumble of a boiler firing in one of the cupboards was loud in the silence that followed. The small room contained two toilet cubicles with the doors missing. The remaining space had a partition dividing off a shower area from a couple of pegs and a bench with distorted wooden slats. Mould grew in cracks between discoloured white tiles.

Dana put her wet clothes on the bench and tip-toed over the grotty floor tiles. The shower was operated by hot and cold taps. The hot tap was missing, and after some consternation, Dana found a pair of pliers on the floor, which she managed to use to operate it.

When she turned the cold tap, water fusilladed from the shower, making the pipes vibrate and rattle against the wall, and for a horrible moment Dana thought the plumbing was going to explode. The noise stopped and the water from the shower settled to a steady stream. She adjusted the taps until the water was hot enough.

A sodden grey flannel lay discarded on the floor, another hanging from a water pipe. Dana touched neither of them. A slimy cake of soap balanced on a cold water pipe above. There wasn't any shampoo. Dana's hair was tangled from not having been combed for three days, and washing it with soap made it worse.

She stood under the hot water, trying to oust the cold that had settled deep in her flesh. After she turned the shower off she tip-toed back to where she had left the towel and dried herself. The clothes Pilgrennon had given her were similar to what Alpha and Peter wore: an old T-shirt, dark leggings and a turtleneck jersey, and a tunic made from an army jacket.

All the clothes as well as the towel smelt faintly like mushrooms. All of them showed seams and evidence of repairs. Dana found the penknife Jananin had given her in her bag to cut the label out of the T-shirt as best as she could. When she put the turtleneck shirt on over it, she grimaced at how itchy it felt on her arms. At least there were pockets in the clothes to put her fuses in.

The boots he'd given her looked like army surplus, and they were too big. She sat on the bench and tied them up, overlapping the leather and winding the laces around the tops.

Dana went to the door and opened it a crack. She looked left and right, seeing no-one.

She closed the door silently and returned to the bag. She checked the pouch she had put the cyanide in, making sure the glass wasn't damaged and it had not got wet.

She picked up the bag and went back to the door. She faced the hall she'd come from, sensing movement behind. It was Pilgrennon, apparently in the act of walking past a door in a room at the end of the corridor. Dana started.

"I see you worked out the hot tap. Sorry, forgot to mention that. Oh." He noticed Dana's bag. "Did that get wet? Want me to wash it for you?"

"No!" Pilgrennon's face changed as her grip tightened on the bag. "It's got my computer in it." Heat rose to her face. What was she going to do if he demanded she give him the bag to inspect?

"Okay, then." He opened a door opposite the one to the shower room and toilets. "I was using this room as a study, but you can have it for the time being. Leave your stuff in here."

The room contained a bed with a metal frame and a brown tattered blanket against the back wall, a handbasin, and a desk with electronics components strewn over its surface. The chair in front of it had been smashed and lay in bits on the floor.

"I'm sorry about the mess."

Dana put the bag under the bed.

"This is the control room." Pilgrennon opened a door at the end of the corridor. Dana leaned past him to see. Unlike the other rooms, the walls and ceiling of the control room were painted white. It contained four office-type chairs. One wall extended to consoles with banks of switches and dead LEDs. Mugs and pieces of paper cluttered them.

"I'll tell you about it later." He turned back down the corridor in the direction they'd come. "That's Peter's room, formerly the barracks, and that's my room, probably an officer's quarters." He pointed to other doors.

"The barracks?" said Dana. "The officer's quarters?"

"Roareim — that's the island," Pilgrennon jerked his thumb up at the ceiling as he glanced down at her. "It's an old disused military base."

He led Dana back into the hall where they had eaten and through a third door from there. This room was warm, with a cast-iron stove, a battered fridge, and a worksurface with a sink. Several worn floor bolsters, some shedding stuffing, clustered to one side near a bookcase and a chess set on a table.

In the far corner stood a rectangular glass box filled with water and rocks. A low bubbling sound came from it, and Peter stood before it. He pushed the black plastic lid back from the top and dropped in some flaky substance from a discoloured plastic pot. A blue-spotted, frog-faced fish with bright red antlers swam to the surface from under a rock. "That's Susan." Peter looked over his shoulder at Dana's entrance.

"Thank you for helping me with the washing up, Peter. Perhaps you can show the fish to Dana tomorrow." He pulled a small book out of his breast pocket. "This is for you, but I want you to read it in your room because I need to talk to Dana for a bit."

Peter's mouth broke into a wide grin as he examined the cover of the book. He turned without speaking and left the room.

Pilgrennon gesticulated at the chess table. "Have a seat."

Dana shuffled the chair forward, putting her knees under the table, her unfamiliar clothing uncomfortable. Pilgrennon reached up to the top of a cupboard and retrieved a foil-wrapped rectangle. He unwrapped the object, which turned out to be a bar of chocolate, and broke off a piece and handed it to Dana.

"Well, now, Dana." Pilgrennon leaned back in his chair and closed his eyes. The chairs were the same folding metal sort they'd sat on for the meal, too small to accommodate his broad frame well. "I've rehearsed this conversation a thousand times, but that doesn't make it any easier. I expect you want to know the meaning of the mast outside, and why you were drawn to it." He opened his eyes, his sight locking with hers. "Ever since I was exiled here, I've nurtured the hope that you, or one of the others, might come."

Dana sniffed the chocolate suspiciously. White marks bloomed on its surface. "The others? My brother, Cale?"

"Your brother? So you know you have a brother. It's good to know they didn't separate you. Tell me about yourself and Cale."

Dana shrugged, unsure what she was supposed to say, thinking only that she must not say anything about Jananin Blake or the cyanide, or why she'd come here.

"Too difficult?" Pilgrennon pointed to the chess set arranged on the table in front of him. "Why don't you show me, then? Pick the chess piece you think is most like you."

Dana looked at the chess pieces. "That's not how you play chess. John showed me once, a bit."

Pilgrennon smiled. "Okay, then. How about you show me how to play chess?"

"I don't remember."

He pressed a switch on the side of the board. Red LEDs flickered around the perimeter squares.

Sensing a signal, Dana drew her head back. "It's a computer?"

"Yes, a very simple, old one. It can play chess, and that's all." Pilgrennon folded his arms, stuck out his bottom lip, and twisted one of his eyebrows to a quizzical angle. "Can you guess how to play chess?"

Dana stared intently at the board, asking it what its purpose was. "You're meant to move one of these bits, and then the computer moves one of another colour. There's a bug in the program."

"Is there?"

Each colour had one piece with a vertical cross on the top — the king. "Yes. If you arrange the pieces in certain ways, that piece will be trapped and the computer will have a fatal error and crash."

"And that's the object of the game."

"To make the computer crash?"

"Yes. You want to see if you can beat the computer?"

Dana reached out and moved a pawn two squares forward. Lights flashed, indicating the square on which the computer's knight sat, and another square. Pilgrennon moved the piece to where the computer instructed.

Dana's pawn had freed up a hole for the bishop to come out. She moved it to the middle of the board. The computer made it known that it wished for a pawn to one side of the king to be moved. Pilgrennon moved it. Dana spotted the gap it had made, and moved the bishop into position to intercept the king. The computer crashed.

"Well," said Pilgrennon. "I've never seen the computer fall for that before. That's fool's mate, smothered mate, and checkmate in one."

"The computer likes me," said Dana. "It wanted to lose. Poor computer." She switched it off.

Pilgrennon started to laugh in a raucous sort of way, making Dana feel uneasy. He wiped his eyes. "So. Can you pick a chess piece to represent you?"

Dana looked at the chessmen, their uniformity, their order, how they were meant to be together as a family.

"None of the chess pieces are like me."

Ivor picked up a white pawn. "We can draw faces on them and colour them in with felt-tip pens, if you like, to make them more individual."

Dana put her hand in her pocket and took out a 3A and a 2A fuse. She set them standing upright in the centre of the board.

"That's me, and that's my brother."

Ivor Pilgrennon interlocked his fingers on his lap and drew his eyebrows down in contemplation. When he offered nothing else, Dana began to consider the other chess pieces. Many of them had obviously been broken and glued back together. The horde of pawns reminded her of the children at school, and the bishops with their upright formality reminded her of Miss Robinson. She took them all off the board and put them on the floor.

She selected the two white rooks and stood them by the two fuses. The knight was a funny piece. John had explained to her how it moved, two spaces straight and one diagonal. She put that next to the rooks and the fuses. She put the two black rooks on the edge of the board. Ivor Pilgrennon observed this without speaking. She gathered the remaining pieces and put them in a heap on her lap.

"So," said Pilgrennon, after she made no further additions. "This is Dana and this is Cale. Who are these other people?"

Dana pointed to the white rooks and knight. "Pauline and Graeme. And Duncan. That's who we live with." She pointed to the black rooks. "That's John and Mary. Before we lived with Pauline and Graeme and Duncan, we lived with John and Mary, and before that, we were with Beatrix. She was horrible."

"That's why she's not on the board?"

"Yes. John and Mary were nice. But social services took them away from us." Dana was squeezing one of the chessmen in her hand as she talked. When she looked down at it, she recognised it as the black queen. This was the most powerful piece. She remembered John explaining to her how the queen could move both diagonally and on the straights. Dana stood the queen on the far corner of the board.

"And who's that?"

"Someone else."

Pilgrennon smiled. "Can I be a chessman? Can you choose me one?"

Dana looked at the pieces remaining in her lap. The kings were the biggest pieces, the most like a tall man, so she selected the white king. She handed it to him. He put it down on the board next to the fuses, opposite the white rooks and the knight. "So, this is me. I'm delighted to meet you and your brother. What does Cale like?"

Dana took a deep breath. "Cale likes tapioca pudding. And he likes the number Pi and he likes insects."

"And what do you like?"

"I like plants. I've got two cacti on my windowsill at Pauline and Graeme's house. Their names are *Myrtillocactus geometrizans* and *Gymnocalycium bruchii*. And I like playing games on the computer with Duncan. I like wLANs and GPS. And I like fuses." Dana put her hand back into her pocket and took out the remaining 13A fuse to show him.

She told him some more about Pauline and Graeme's garden and the names of plants in it, and how she was looking forward to it being spring and the plants growing again, and about fuses in plugs and how there seemed to be a lot of plugs that wanted 13A and 2A and 3A fuses, but not fuses of the other amperages. Throughout, he listened to her, nodding occasionally, and he didn't, like a lot of people do, interrupt with a forcible question unrelated to what Dana was talking about, or tell her to stop going on about plants and fuses.

"When you and your brother were born, I called him Delta and you Epsilon." Pilgrennon rubbed his eye. "Those are Greek letters. I'm not much good with names. There was a Gamma as well, but as you can see she hasn't found this place. Not yet, anyway." The man flashed a quick, nervous smile.

Dana swallowed and kept her voice calm. "There is a piece of metal in my head."

Pilgrennon began to rearrange the chessmen to their starting positions in a ponderous, meticulous sort of way. "Correct. There're pieces of metal in Alpha's and Peter's heads, and in Cale's head, and in Gamma's head, wherever and whoever she might be. You all use them to various degrees of efficacy. You, I suspect, use yours rather better than any other of my children."

"Your children?"

Pilgrennon sighed. "In a way, yes." He leaned forward

and clasped his hands between his knees. "Dana, what I am going to tell you is difficult. You must be aware that I have done some things of which I am not proud regarding you and your brother and those children we have just eaten with."

Pilgrennon did not look at Dana for a few moments. He toyed with the knight. "Do you know how these work?"

Dana shrugged. Pilgrennon picked up the knight and turned it so its base pointed towards her, showing a device embedded in it. "Infra red," he said, waving it slowly back and forth in front of her forehead. He put the knight back. "Now play again, without the computer."

"I don't understand. How can it work without the computer?"

"I'm going to be the computer. Come along then, white moves first."

Dana moved a pawn. Pilgrennon also moved a pawn. Dana felt confused. She couldn't remember how the pieces were supposed to move. She moved another pawn. Pilgrennon did something with his bishop. Dana moved the first pawn again.

"A-a!" Pilgrennon put out his hand. "They can only move two squares on their first move."

Dana moved the pawn back a square. Pilgrennon moved the bishop again, setting it down with a conclusive force. Dana wondered about what to move next, but realised her king was trapped and the black bishop was aimed at it.

Pilgrennon leaned back on his chair and interlocked his fingers behind his head. "I just beat you," he said, "using the *exact* same moves you used to beat the computer."

"How?"

"My guess? You understood what the computer was doing the first time. The second time," he tapped his right temple with his index finger, "you were playing against me, and you can't tell what I'm thinking. You see, Dana, this computer was never meant to convey its intentions by its IR position detector mechanism, but the IR signal is a signal you can understand, and you used it to make the computer tell you things, and you understood it like *that!*" He snapped his fingers. "Even though you had never seen it before. Don't you think that's amazing?"

"Because of the thing in my head?"

"Yes, yes." He looked Dana in the face. "You no doubt have received a formal diagnosis of autism by now."

Dana thought again of the cyanide in the backpack, but she nodded silently.

Pilgrennon started fiddling with a rook. "I'm a psychologist and a geneticist — that's a sort of scientist. My field of research is — was — autistic spectrum disorders. I used to have a facility in Oxford. We looked after autistic children there. I wanted to help autistic children to lead normal lives."

He leaned his elbow on his knee and scratched his cheek, nails rasping on stubble. "I discovered that nearly all autistic children have this natural... *affinity*, for computers. I found even the most insular children would open their minds, engage, when left alone with a computer. I started trying to come up with better interfaces for the children at my facility to use. You see, at the time, the instruments people used to communicate with computers were keyboards and mice. Autistic children were capable of so much using computers, but they were held back by these interfaces."

Yes, Jananin had told Dana that Pilgrennon studied autism.

Pilgrennon breathed deeply. "I learned of a chemical someone had invented that could connect the bits that make up a human brain to the bits that make up computers. So I paid for the rights to use this chemical, and I designed a device that could relay information to and from a kind of wireless network that was becoming popular."

Dana tried to keep her voice under control. "A *device?* You put this thing in my head?"

Creases formed on Pilgrennon's forehead. "Dana, it has been a long time since I have had, well, I suppose, an *adult* conversation. My past actions have been a burden upon my conscience in my years here on Roareim, and it has not been made easier by solitude. Peter and Alpha are both older than you, but I sense that you are more mature than them in a number of ways."

He put his hand back on the rook and tilted it from side to side, eyes fixed on his fingers. "Undoubtedly, you came here for answers. It would be very easy to lie and invent an explanation for my exile here. But you found a way here yourself, and I believe you deserve better."

Pilgrennon shifted in his seat. "We tried it on Alpha, but it... you've seen what happened to Alpha. I decided it was safer to test it on foetuses. A foetus is what grows inside a pregnant woman and eventually becomes a baby."

Dana didn't entirely follow this. "Where does the foetus come from?"

Pilgrennon looked a bit flustered. "A man and a woman..."

"I know *that*," said Dana.

"And that makes a baby."

"Do they do that before or after the foetus is there?"

"The foetus that grows into a baby is a combination of the man and the woman. It grows into a foetus and then it grows into a baby and gets born."

"So you took a foetus out of a woman?"

Pilgrennon twisted a gold ring on the third finger of his left hand. "No, the foetus was still inside the woman. a foetus can't live by itself until it becomes a baby and is born. It's a technique called keyhole surgery. Just after the foetus's brain had begun to develop, we inserted the device I had made between the two halves of the brain and injected the chemical into the surrounding tissue.

"I implanted four foetuses with the implants: you and Cale, Beta — he likes to be called Peter now — and Gamma. And you were all born healthy, and the experiment was a success." He smiled awkwardly.

"If I was an experiment that was a success, why did you leave me on Vine Street?" Dana said, rather louder than she had meant to.

Pilgrennon grasped his queen, squeezing it until his knuckles paled. "There was this other scientist, Dr Blake, who invented the chemical that connects your brain up to the device in your head, who told the police about my research."

Dana's breath stuck in her throat. He meant Jananin, she was sure. "Why did she do that?"

One of Pilgrennon's eyebrows twitched slightly. After a moment, he answered: "I paid her a lot of money for the rights to use her invention. We agreed on the amount. But she changed her mind and decided she wanted more money. I didn't have any more. And so she told the police about you and my other children. She made it sound like I had put the devices in your heads to hurt you, and that was never what I meant to do."

Pilgrennon put down the queen and wrung his hands. "I mean, I hurt Alpha, but that was an accident; I was trying to help her. I put that device in your head so that you could have some protection against other people who will treat you badly because of your difference. But the only thing Blake wanted was more money. The police came to raid my laboratory, so I blew it up and ran away. Alpha and Peter were old enough for me to take them with me. But it wasn't safe to bring children as young as you and your brother to this place." Pilgrennon spread his arms wide. "You would have died of hypothermia. So I had to give you up. I decided you were better off cared for in a real family."

"I'm not in a real family," said Dana. "Pauline and

Graeme are foster parents."

Pilgrennon shrugged. "I'm sorry to hear that. Of course, it was always my intention to care for you and your brother as my own, before Blake decided to intervene. That's why I put the transmitter on the mast up on the island, to help you find this place, had you wanted to, when you were old enough and capable enough to do so, and it seems it has served its purpose. If you decide you'd like to stay here I'm perfectly happy to allow it. But of course," he lowered his head briefly, keeping his eyes fixed on her, "that must be your own decision. If you'd prefer to return to your foster family, I can arrange that instead."

Dana pushed her feet against the stem of the table. "Where is the woman I was a foetus inside?"

"Her name was Jade. Jade Cooper." Pilgrennon rose and fetched a file from the bookcase. He opened it and leafed through some documents inside. "Yes. This is what doctors call an ultrasound scan. It's a special machine that lets you look inside a woman who's pregnant and see the foetuses. There's you and your brother in the picture, see?" He turned the square of card around with thick, oddly dextrous fingers and placed it on the table in front of Dana.

The things in the picture were pressed closely together, interlocking like a yin-yan symbol. They looked like prawns in the process of turning into people, with bunched-up limbs and dark bulbous eyes. Lodged in the front of each bulging forehead was a dark, dense mass with a solid outline.

"Is that really the thing in my brain?" Dana exclaimed, bringing her fingers to her forehead.

"Yes." Pilgrennon smiled. "You and Cale used to talk to each other — with the devices in your heads, I mean — while you were inside Jade. They didn't come across as words or anything, they were just radionoise that we picked up with our equipment when we were scanning her. And you used to talk to the computers. I'd be sitting typing and Jade would come into the room, and long strings of random text would write themselves on the screen."

"I don't remember," said Dana.

"Nobody ever does. All the things people do as foetuses and when they're very young are to help set their brains up to work properly when they get older. You have to learn how to see, how to hear, how to control how your body moves. And in your case, how to use the device in your head. I think you simply don't remember your life inside your mother because you hadn't yet learnt how to remember."

"Who was Jade?"

"She was someone who had problems. We helped her stop taking drugs and find a job, and gave her a safe place to have her babies."

"So she was my mother?"

Pilgrennon arched his eyebrows and gave a slight nod. "Yes."

"Then where is she now?"

"I'm sorry but I don't know. She wasn't in a position to look after you, and she left not long after you and Cale were born."

Dana stared at Pilgrennon, then at the chocolate on the chess board.

"I understand this might be hard for you to understand. It's late, and all this will no doubt seem a lot clearer after you've slept." Pilgrennon stood and stretched, leaning back and pushing his hands into the arch of his back. "As I've said, you're welcome to stay here if that's what you decide you want. There's no rush, and you can decide tomorrow."

The enormity of the conflict in what Dana had heard started turning over in her head as soon as Pilgrennon went to open the kitchen door.

Pilgrennon had said he'd put the device in her head

to help her. And she supposed the device did help her. He hadn't meant her to be in a school where Abigail would attack her; he hadn't meant her and Cale to end up in foster care. It wasn't his fault.

And if Dana didn't belong in that world, perhaps she would belong in Pilgrennon's world. Perhaps he would be like her dad. She looked at him nervously once more, averting her eyes lest he catch her in the act. His curly hair — her and Cale's hair was a bit curly — and the way he had stuck his bottom lip out when they were playing chess reminded her of how Cale used to look when he was thinking. Suddenly she wanted so hard for what Pilgrennon had told her to be true, for her to have been born because he wanted her to be, and to belong somewhere.

That wasn't what Jananin had said.

But Pilgrennon had said Dana's mother's name was Jade Cooper. Jananin claimed she was Dana's mother. And Pilgrennon had said that Doctor Blake — that was Jananin's name, wasn't it? — had blackmailed him for money.

It wasn't what Jananin had said.

Could Jananin be Dana's mother? She had the same colour hair as Dana. But then lots of people who weren't related to Dana had dark hair. Perhaps Dana had only noticed it because Jananin said. Jananin had known Pilgrennon was here and about the beacon. Should she tell Pilgrennon what Jananin had said to her? No; that was a bad idea. If he found out about the cyanide he might not like her any more, and then what if it turned out Jananin was right? But what Ivor had said made sense, didn't it?

But if Ivor Pilgrennon was just someone Jananin was trying to get money off of, why did she want Dana to poison him?

Dana stared at Pilgrennon's broad back and his shabby clothes. He didn't look like the James Bond baddy she'd imagined. He certainly didn't behave like one, inviting her to dinner and to play chess with him. She'd expected him to wear a suit and be thin and wiry with a shock of silver hair. Did he look like someone who stole people's gametes? How did one steal gametes anyway? Perhaps they come out when you go to the toilet. Perhaps it had been as harmless as Jananin leaving her pencil on a desk and Pilgrennon coming by, thinking, *What a nice pencil,* and putting it in his pocket, and Jananin seeing him writing with it later and accusing him, *That's my pencil! You stole it!*

But then why had Pilgrennon not *said?*

She couldn't make sense of any of this. It was as though both of them had said the opposite thing to the other. Perhaps, as Pilgrennon had said, it would be clearer by morning.

A horned human form — Peter — loitered near the door of the room Pilgrennon had assigned to her as they went back into the corridor. He swung on the doorframe and asked, "Is Dana going to stay with us then, Ivor?"

-10-

WHEN Dana lay in the hazy void between sleeping and waking, she could have been anywhere. In the warmth, with the bedcover over her head, this could be the musty spare bedroom in Jananin's bleak stone house, or her bed in Graeme and Pauline's home, if not for the absence of the feeling of Cale nearby. And Pilgrennon had been right: the disturbed confusion his words had given her had passed. It no longer mattered.

Perhaps Ivor Pilgrennon had stolen Jananin Blake's gametes; perhaps Jananin had wronged him back by demanding money from him and telling the police about what he had done. It felt easier not to care now.

The lamp on the table beside her bed started to glow dimly. She lay studying the discoloured patterns on the concrete ceiling. When there were no other noises, the silence of the rock gave way to a very low booming sound, probably something to do with the sea.

A scratching sound alerted her. Dana sat up in bed and looked at the door. It opened slowly. Peter stood on the other side, wearing a grey dressing gown with his horned helmet.

"Your hair is sticking up by itself." He didn't come into the room, standing behind the door and staring with round, curious eyes.

"Hello Peter." Dana got up and put on a similar dark-grey towelling dressing gown and the cloth slippers she'd been given. "Do you wear your hat in bed?"

"Oh, that?" Peter touched his helmet. "No. I can take it off in my room with the door shut, but Ivor says I'm not allowed to anywhere else because I mess things up."

"What things do you mess up?"

"Them." Peter pointed at the electronics components on the desk. "That." He moved his hand to point at the broken chair. "I have ants in my pants."

Dana looked Peter up and down.

Peter giggled. "They're not real ants. It's just something Ivor says."

Peter skipped off in the direction of the room with the broken ceiling they'd eaten in the day before. Dana followed him into the kitchen, where he stood on a chair to inspect his fish. Peter jumped from the chair to one of the other chairs near the chess table, jumped off, and sat on one of the bolsters, picking up a book that had been lying on the floor.

"What are you reading?"

"Fish."

Dana's clothes hung drying on a rack near the iron stove whose radiating heat warmed the little kitchen.

That feeling again, like when Cale was near. Dana glanced back to the door, and Pilgrennon entered with Alpha behind him. He wore an Iron Maiden T-shirt and a pair of pyjama trousers under a burgundy dressing gown, worn thin at the elbows. His formerly tidy hair had become greasy and dishevelled.

"Ah, Dana. I hope you didn't find the mattress too uncomfortable. Alpha, sit down." He tied up the belt on his dressing gown. "I wouldn't touch the Aga. It gets very hot and you might hurt yourself." He picked up a metal kettle, filled it, and lifted up one of the covers on the stove to set it down. He took a potato out of a bag under one of the worksurfaces and started grating it up, without peeling it. "Perhaps you would like to see the island today, Dana." Pilgrennon watched her as he arranged some pieces of meat on a tray.

"Yes, please," said Dana politely.

He smiled briefly, raised his eyebrows, and tipped the grated-up potatoes into a frying pan. He stood watching them and twisting the gold ring on the third finger of his left hand. Graeme had a ring like that, and he used to fiddle with it as well. Sometimes he would start sliding it on and off different fingers, and Pauline would get cross with him.

A sudden shrill whistle and a geyser of steam startled Dana, and she clapped hands to ears. Pilgrennon picked up the kettle, which hissed as water slopped about inside it. He put some brown powder into a teapot and poured the water in with it. "Do you like tea?"

"Yes," said Dana. "But that's coffee."

The man picked up the jar the brown powder had come from and showed it to Dana. It smelt like tea.

"What's tea supposed to look like?" he asked.

"It comes in circles," said Dana, confused.

"Those are tea bags. This is the tea that's inside the tea bags." Pilgrennon put the lid on the teapot and pulled a knitted tea cosy over it. "I don't have any sugar, but you can have some UHT milk in it if you like." He opened the fridge door and brandished a carton. He fetched four unmatching mugs from a cupboard and poured milk into them, and gave the sizzling pan of potato gratings a prod with a fork. After swirling the teapot a bit, he poured it into the four mugs through a small sieve. He set down the teapot and placed one mug in her hands, with a flourish and a sort of bow, as though serving it to someone important. "There you are."

Dana sat a floor cushion near Peter, while Pilgrennon gave a mug each to Peter and Alpha. He took the pan off the hob and chopped up the clod of fried potato, dividing it between four plates. The pieces of meat from the oven and some more leaves from the fridge joined it. Dana put her mug on the floor as he handed her a plate and fork.

Dana poked the meat. "What's this?"

"Seagull, Milady."

She put some in her mouth. It tasted oily and fishy.

What was that feeling? Dana looked at Alpha. A sudden change overcame the girl: Alpha stared at the hand she held her fork in, as though it did not belong to her and some force not of her own controlled its actions. Slowly, unsteadily, she raised her face, until her round, blank eyes looked straight back at Dana.

Dana started and her breakfast slid off her knee with a clang. "Oops," Pilgrennon chuckled, as he lunged to arrest it and missed. "Never mind, I think the floor's fairly clean." He picked up the food and put it back on the plate, and set it on Dana's knee.

Dana chewed her food mechanically and forced herself to swallow against the sensation in the pit of her stomach, concentrating fiercely on her plate, not looking up at Alpha again. She did not belong here, and if Pilgrennon found out Jananin had sent her here to kill him, there was no telling what might happen. In that instant, she had felt vulnerable. Could Alpha somehow see into Dana's mind? Something about Alpha was not right. Alpha was nothing like any of the children Dana had encountered at school or in care placements. She had her own signal, like Cale, but Dana couldn't sense her thinking behind it, like she could with Cale. It was as though she was sleepwalking.

Peter put his plate on the floor when he had finished. Dana wondered if he too could see through this. For a dreadful instant, the idea occurred that Pilgrennon himself and both of them knew, and he led them all on a merry masquerade that could only end in doom. Jananin had said he studied autistic children. What if her every movement gave her intentions away, like that 'body language' thing she had some vague perception of normal people using to tell each other things secretly. Heat prickled under her skin. She could not look up at their faces!

Ivor stacked his plate on top of Peter's and slapped his thick knees vigorously. "If you'd like to have a shower, you can go first and Peter and I will go afterwards."

He nudged Dana before she realised he had been

addressing her. When she looked up his eyes bored into her face, and it was all she could do to stop herself from panicking again like she had done in the school when the wLAN failed.

"I'm okay, I had a shower yesterday."

"You get to miss things, living here," Pilgrennon said as he got up. "Baths is one of 'em." Soon after he'd gone, Peter put down his book and followed him.

Dana stacked her plate as the others had done and picked up the book. Watery stains marked dog-eared pages, and Peter's hands had smudged the cover. *Tropical Marine Aquaria*, by Graham F. Cox. Dana frowned: the people who had printed the book had spelled *Graeme* wrong. The page where Peter had left it open showed round, fantastic-looking fish, with colours too bright for Dana to believe real. She carefully put the book back, propping it open as Peter had left it.

"Do you want a shower, Alpha?" Dana asked. Alpha didn't respond. Dana watched her for a few minutes, but all she did was sit there and breathe.

Dana went back to her room and washed her face and cleaned her teeth in the sink there, and got dressed.

Peter had said the things on the desk were from appliances he'd broken. Dana knew the little coloured plastic things came from inside computers, although she didn't know what they did. She picked one of them up: it was yellow, with 25 W written on it in tiny black letters. Another one was a flattened black cuboid with many legs, like a centipede, and a transparent circle on its back.

Impulsively, Dana opened the drawer on the desk. A pen weighed down a few sheets of printed paper. She noticed the corners had been well thumbed when she took the paper out.

Young genius wins Nobel Prize

Dr Jananin Blake was yesterday awarded the Nobel Prize for her research in semiconducting biological molecules. Dr Blake's work over the past year at Cambridge University culminated in the development of a 'biological wire' capable of attaching to brain cells in laboratory animal tests, which she hopes can be put to use as a revolutionary new connection medium to prosthetic limbs in amputees. Blake's research may well herald the dawn of a new age of true bionic technology. At 27, Dr Blake is the youngest individual to be awarded the prize.

Dana sat on the bed and looked at the picture in the top corner of the article, trying to match the face to her memory of Jananin. It must have been taken more than ten years ago. The black-and-white pixels showed an unsmiling young woman, her face somehow made cruel by the two-dimensional printing process.

She lifted up a few of the documents in the drawer. One of them was written in two columns, the words mostly scientific terminology she couldn't understand. The document consisted of seven or eight sheets of A4 stapled together. The top left read *Journal of the American Chemical Society*, and the title on the first page was *Semiconducting properties of novel DNA analogues, J. Blake*, and below, *University of Cambridge*.

Why would Jananin's work be in a journal about American chemistry? Jananin wasn't American. Cambridge wasn't in America, was it? It was so difficult to know where anything was without GPS or a wLAN.

As she turned to the next document, a rectangle of cheap paper of the sort used for printing tabloid newspapers slipped from between the sheets and fluttered to the floor. Dana picked it up.

MAD SCIENTIST SAYS NO

Nobel prizewinner Janine Blake has declined an offer of six million pounds from company Flexicon for her invention of a device that might be used to connect the human brain to a robot. Flexicon what manufactures replacement arms and legs says millions of patients they could have helped will continue to suffer because of Miss Blakes decision. Fred Sullivan is one such person. Fred who lost the use of his legs in a building sight accident said to The Sun 'Blake is a heartless cow. She doesnt care about people. All she wants is to exploit her discoveries for money. These scientists sit in there ivory towels, deciding who can and who cant have access to medical technology.' Flexicon managers have still not decided weather or not they are going to make a higher offer.

Dana leapt to her feet at a knock on the door. She shoved the papers back into the drawer as Ivor Pilgrennon entered, wearing an RAF jacket. He held out her coat. "Your jacket, Madam. It seems to have dried off nicely."

Ivor took Dana to see the place down at the shore where the lobster traps were. He showed her the path up to the top of the island and the place where he grew dandelions, which Dana told him were called *Taraxacum officinale*. On the top of the island stood a tall mast, and at the top of this was the transmitter that gave off the buzzing, colour-shifting signal she'd followed all the way out here, and a windmill that generated electricity and a number of photovoltaic panels.

Boxes lay scattered about the grass for trapping rabbits. One of them had a rabbit in it, and Ivor pulled its neck and skinned and gutted it because, he said, it tasted better than seagull. He turned his back on Dana when he did it so she didn't see, but he left its discarded innards steaming on the grass, and she wondered if he'd do the same thing to her if he found out she'd been sent here to poison him.

Dana looked down at the waves breaking on the rocks below. "What is this place? I know it's called the Flannan Isles, but I can't find it on GPS."

"GPS?" Pilgrennon smiled at Dana. "I did wonder if you would learn how to use it. Peter can sense it, and use it to an extent, but he gets agitated by it sometimes. This island is called Roareim, but I wouldn't be surprised if it wasn't on GPS maps. After all, no roads go here."

"Do you like living here?"

He shrugged. "I suppose, if you like to be sociable, and to have a high-flying career, and to go out drinking and to fancy restaurants, and for everything to be new, and tidy, and scrupulously clean, you wouldn't like living here. But if you like solitude, and nature, and foraging for your own food, and fresh air, and reading, then you would like living here. And I like it very much."

He bent over and leant towards her. "Come here and I'll show you." He hoisted her up onto his shoulder as though she hardly weighed anything. The wind whipped her hair up. Dana gripped the collar of his jacket; she trusted neither his grip nor her sense of balance.

Ivor pointed down over Roareim's edge, and Dana recognised the eerie rock stacks. "That little island over there is called Bròna Cleit. The bigger island," his finger traced along the smattering of sea-ravaged rocks, "is Eilean a' Ghobha." He pronounced the words with a forcedly thick, rolling Scottish accent that made Dana laugh. "Those are Gaelic words."

He shuffled his feet to face back west, shrugging his shoulder so Dana lurched up in the air. "The island with the lighthouse is Eilean Mór, and the one next to it, Eilean Tighe. 'Eilean' means 'island'. Those other islands on the right, I forget which is which. They all look like one from here, anyway. The one in the middle is Toman. You must've come from Lewis, I suppose. The bit of Lewis that sticks out farthest this way is called Gallan Head."

"I went there."

"Then you'll know it's an abandoned Ministry of Defence site. That site was built around the same time the base was dug under this rock, during the Second World War."

"What for?"

"Well, the one at Gallan Head was for a communications array. I've never managed to work out what the one here was meant for. Obviously, it was intended to be hidden, so its existence was probably never made public in the first place. When I found it, it had been derelict for decades. The roof in the hall had fallen in, and much of the furniture that's there now had been packed away in cupboards. They probably had no need of it when the war ended, and they just went home. There are very few people left who were alive during the Second World War. It's quite likely that there is nobody in the world left who knew about this place or what, indeed, it was made for."

Dana felt precarious balancing on his shoulder; the ground seemed a long way down. Ivor must surely be one of the tallest, strongest men in the world.

He held Dana a few moments longer as she gazed at the faint form of Lewis, before sliding her off his shoulder, his bulk momentarily blocking the wind. Ivor smelt mostly like old army clothes and sweatiness, but there was something else evading her there: something more than just an odour, and it evoked emotions so ancient that at first they would not take the form of words. She remembered they had taken Cale away, and Cale had never been taken away from her before. And this man with big hands had picked her up and held her to his shoulder, and his smell had comforted her. She remembered the tiny, regular quartz *squeak* his watch used to make, and she sensed it again.

"Hey, listen!"

Dana stood still and listened. It wasn't an obvious sound, unless you were searching for it. Above the relentless rush of the swell came a dull, regular throb, like the blades of an enormous fan turning in slow motion.

"What is it?"

"Minke whales. Don't usually hear them in the winter. It must mean spring is just around the corner. And spring means the puffins come to nest, and puffin-egg omelettes."

"Can you eat puffin eggs?"

"You can eat any bird egg. And probably reptile and amphibian eggs too, if you want. And sea birds, and seaweed, fish, crustaceans. The sea provides." He breathed in a deep draught of air, and then, unexpectedly, he hugged her to him. Dana didn't really like physical contact with other people, whether she knew them well or not, but she didn't mind it too much this time, and she leaned against him and tried to recall something not quite within memory, a feeling that was very still, that made the thought of Abigail and the school, and what Jananin Blake had said to her about him, seem very distant and unimportant.

He released her and smiled down at her. "I'm sorry, Dana, if I seem like a sentimental old sod. It's just it is *wonderful* to meet you at last and get to know the person you've become."

Back inside, they made a lunch of potatoes and fried rabbit meat. Dana helped do the salad and Ivor juggled with the potatoes. After they had sat down to lunch, and Ivor had told Alpha to eat hers, Peter asked with his mouth full, "Is Dana going to stay with us?"

"Like I said yesterday, that's Dana's choice to make."

Peter stared intently at Dana, and Dana glanced between him and Pilgrennon. "I don't know," she said. "I want to go back to my brother, and I like living with Pauline and Graeme and Duncan. But when I've liked living with people before, like John and Mary, they've been taken away from us. And they make me go to a school, and I hate it. And I think they want me to go back to the hospital, about this thing in my head. I don't know if they are going to take it out."

Dana picked at the remainder of her meal. When Ivor asked her if she'd had enough, she put the plate down on the floor, and he divided what she'd left between Peter's plate and his own.

After they'd cleared up the pots, Ivor took out some

sheets of A4 paper from a pile in the bookcase and a pencil box. "Dana, perhaps you could draw something, to help you understand how you're feeling? Peter, you can play this game too, if you want."

Peter came and sat at the chess table. Dana took the seat opposite him. Ivor cleared away the chessmen and put a piece of paper in front of each of them. "Now," he said, taking a ruler and pencil and dividing Dana's page in half horizontally and in thirds vertically, so it was split into six boxes. "Draw three things you would miss if you didn't live where you live now, and three things you wouldn't miss."

Dana quite liked drawing, although she wasn't as good at it as Cale. Opposite her, Peter began a vigorous scribbly illustration. Pilgrennon took another piece of paper and spoke to Alpha. He got her to sit down on one of the floor cushions and he put a pencil into her fingers in the right position. But Alpha's fingers wouldn't hold the pencil, and he had to hold them against it and sit beside her with his arm around her. When he put her hand to the paper, speaking calmly to her all along, she didn't try to use it, and he had to guide her hand.

When he finished helping Alpha, he came over to the table to see what Dana and Peter had drawn. He turned Peter's drawing so Dana could see it too.

Peter had drawn in the top boxes a man and two girls, a rectangle containing fish, and a picture of an island in the sea. In the bottom boxes, he'd drawn a man and a boy sitting at a table, the boy in a Viking helmet and presumably intended to be himself, the same man and boy facing each other, and a figure with a Viking helmet and a beard aboard a Viking ship with a dragon's head on its prow.

Peter explained: "If I didn't live here, I would miss Ivor and Alpha and Dana. I would miss my fish, and I would miss Roareim."

"Very good, Peter," Ivor said. "And what about what

you wouldn't miss?"

"Well, I wouldn't miss your cooking, especially when it's eels or mussels, and I wouldn't miss being told what I can't do. And if I didn't live here and I was older, I thought I could grow a beard and build my own ship. I would make a ship with a sail like that, because yours has a motor and it keeps on breaking, so it's not very reliable."

Pilgrennon laughed and patted Peter on the back. "Very good. Although, that last one is maybe a *fantasy* about what you *could do* rather than something you would *miss*. And you do understand that, if I tell you not to do something, like that you're not allowed to go outside and play on the island when it's dark or when boats are passing, it's for your own good?"

Peter gave a weary and drawn-out reply of, "Yes."

"How about you, Dana?" Pilgrennon pushed Peter's paper back to him and turned Dana's to look. "Who's this?"

"That's Cale." Dana pointed to the boy she'd drawn in the first box. In the second box, she'd drawn a bigger boy next to a computer. "That's playing computer games with Duncan. And that's a wLAN." In the third box, Dana had drawn a horizontal rectangle to represent the box, with circles on the front where the lights were, and an aerial on one side.

"Ah, now we do have those things, but we have to keep them out of the way, because Peter doesn't get on with them." Pilgrennon glanced at Peter.

Peter said, "Ivor says I am like a bull in a china shop with electronic things."

"So what have you drawn that you won't miss?"

Dana pointed to the bottom row, where she'd drawn a building, an adult with lots of children, and an abstract design made of lines and circles. "The hospital, the teacher and the children at school, and something else. I don't know how to draw it. It's not a thing you can see."

Ivor pulled up another chair and sat between Peter and Dana. He put his hand on Dana's shoulder. "Some things no-one can see, but they're still real. Is it a feeling, an emotion?"

"Maybe." Dana frowned. "It's if I didn't live there, I always thought it would be because social services said I couldn't live with Pauline and Graeme any more, and they decided I had to live with someone else. But when you told me I had to think of something and draw it, I thought it might not be that way. I mean, you said it was up to me to choose. If I wasn't there because I chose to be here, or somewhere else, then it would be... different. I wouldn't miss *not having a choice*."

"That's quite a deep thought." He gave her shoulder a squeeze. "And well articulated! Very good. If you like computers and using the Internet, I might be able to help with that. Peter, are you okay to stay here and look after Alpha, and draw or read quietly for a bit?"

Peter nodded, making a snotty sniff at the same time. "I will draw some more detail on the pictures I already drew."

Ivor led Dana back through the big room and through his bedroom, to a locked door within it. As he found the key to open it, she looked around. A double bed and small metal wardrobe occupied the main part of the room. The rest had been fashioned into a study, with a threadbare armchair, a desk, a scratched-up coffee table, and shelving bolted to the walls. A collection of rocks and different-sized bird skulls arrayed one shelf. Books resided on another, beside two dull conkers.

Some photographs caught Dana's eye — one of a girl, perhaps in her early teenage years, with wavy auburn hair. The one next to it she recognised as being of a younger Pilgrennon, without the glasses he usually wore, standing in a sunny meadow with reddened, freckled cheeks and sun-bleached hair. Grubby marks covered his shirt. He looked plumper, not so haggard. He had his arm around the shoulders of a young, tomboyish woman with choppy light brown hair. Another photograph without a frame, of pale flowers, had been tacked to one wall.

Inside the small room, a table set to one side held a cubic television like the one she had seen in Jananin's house, with a large rectangular object beside it and some other things in front.

"The bulb in here's gone. I need to get some more. Mind the floor," Ivor said.

Dana looked down as she stepped away from the door. Grooves ran over the concrete surface. An old heavy mechanism took up floorspace on the other side to the table.

"Whatever piece of equipment the military had in here, the mounting for it is still attached to the floor."

"Where's the computer?"

"It's here." Ivor showed Dana to a seat in front of the table with the box on it.

"Where?"

He pressed something on the rectangular object. The screen on the box lit up and the word 'loading' appeared.

Ivor sat on a stool and they both stared at the screen until an image emerged that looked more similar to that on a computer screen, with icons lined up.

"How do you work it?" Dana asked.

She heard Ivor chuckle. From the glare of the computer screen, she could not make out much from his face. "Believe me, this was once state of the art!" He picked up Dana's hand and put it down on something on the table. "This is a mouse. I don't know what you use now instead of one. A pen, or something, I suppose." He wiggled the mouse and Dana's hand around. An arrow moved on the screen.

"You can probably manage without using the mouse, anyway." Ivor pointed to something else on the desk with a small green light blinking on it. "This is a WiFi port. It does essentially the same thing as the device in your head. You should be able to control the computer from that."

"I think I can," said Dana. In truth, she had been vaguely aware of something since Ivor had switched the computer on. But if this was the computer, it did not seem to be much of a computer at all. It felt more like Duncan's phone. She started one of the icons on the screen.

"At any rate," said Ivor, "The thing you'll be more interested in is this." He pressed a normal electrical switch low down on the wall, and another object on the floor started flashing a green light.

"It's a wLAN," said Dana.

"Pretty much. You remember the pylon on Roareim that makes the signal you followed to come here?"

"The beacon?"

"Yes, it's not just a beacon. It transmits signals called microwaves. You can't sense the microwaves because it would've been too dangerous for me to have put a microwave device in your brain, but you can detect the signal if it is first converted into another kind of signal, such as the one produced by the wLAN. There's an aerial above this dome, which is plugged directly into that wLAN box there. That picks up the signals from the mast and converts them."

Dana was looking for Jananin's name on the internet. There was information about her on it, but none of it was recent.

"What are you looking at?"

Dana turned sharply to face him.

"The wLAN box. The light flashes when it's conveying data."

"Nothing. I was just checking it worked."

A heavy thump came from behind the door to the bedroom.

"Peter," said Pilgrennon loudly, "You need to calm down. Go and read your fish book."

A loud scream of defiance came from behind the door.

Pilgrennon got up in a hurry. "Dana, you need to understand that Peter sometimes has these moods. He loses his temper and throws things around. I'm going to try to calm him down. If he takes his helmet off, he sometimes gives out signals that hurt Alpha. You can stay here if you want, but keep out the way as I don't want you getting hurt."

He went out, closing the door to the bedroom behind him. Then Dana remembered Jananin's laptop, in the bag in her bedroom, and the cyanide. What if Peter broke the computer, or Ivor found the bag?

Dana ran back into the corridor and to her room. She fumbled in the pockets in the light coming from the doorway. Her fingers touched the cold glass of the vial. She had to get rid of it, or at least hide it somewhere better. She didn't know what to do; she needed more information. She couldn't throw the cyanide away, because then there would be no choice. If Pilgrennon turned out to be the person who had stolen Jananin's gametes, she would never be able to do what Jananin had asked her. She couldn't leave it here, because Pilgrennon might find it, or even worse, Peter might find it and eat it. Then she remembered the groove on the floor in the computer room.

She went back there, to the mechanism to the side of the computer desk. The cyanide bottle fitted neatly into the groove in the floor. She slid it underneath the base of the mechanism. Pilgrennon probably couldn't see things close up without his glasses on, and there was no chance he'd notice it in this light. His hands were too big to get hold of it under there and pull it out. Peter wasn't allowed in here, so it would be safe from him.

She turned back to the computer, deciding to check its internet history. Perhaps there might be some clue about what had happened between Jananin Blake and

Ivor Pilgrennon in that. Every day for the last week, the computer had been used to look at the same website. A government encrypted website, apparently, but it didn't take Dana long to deal with that. There was a picture of an animal with three heads, and the word 'Cerberus', but no links to anything else. Dana could feel a lot of Internet traffic and complicated data moving and changing, like standing behind a screen in front of which innumerable people were passing, and she could see nothing of any of them.

Dana went to a search engine and entered the text 'Cerberus' into the search field. It found hundreds of references. She read the first paragraphs of a few of them. They were all about Greek myths. Cerberus was a three-headed dog in a place called Erebus. Most of the references alluded to other characters as well, such as Hades the god of the underworld and Charon the ferryman.

A series of loud crashes came from somewhere down the corridor. Dana went to the door and looked out. The chairs in the dining area were scattered all over the room. As she went through, she noticed a shape hidden in a crevice in the side of the table, and realised it was Alpha, curled up.

In the kitchen, Peter was no longer wearing his helmet. He was giving off a horrible signal, and Dana could see now how he had managed to break whatever all the components on the desk in her bedroom had come from. He was doing the same thing she had done when she'd panicked and broken the wLAN in Miss Robinson's classroom and the television at the fast food kiosk. He didn't mean to do it; he had just lost control, and he was overloading himself and everything around him.

Peter kicked over the chess table, sending the chessmen flying, and spat in Ivor's face. Ivor caught hold of Peter from behind, in a bear hug that pinioned his arms to his sides. Peter struggled violently, and Ivor sat on a chair, holding him. "Peter, Peter, Peter," he said, in a slow, soothing voice. "*Peter* out."

"Get off me, Ivor!" Peter suddenly bared his teeth and bent his head forward, then swung it backwards with such force the back of his skull hit Ivor on the chin and sent him reeling back. He lost his grip on Peter, who picked up a hardbacked book and hurled it at him.

Dana and Cale had once lived with a woman called Beatrix. She was experienced in caring for autistic children, or so the social worker had said. Also staying with her at the time was a girl called Millie. Millie wasn't nasty like the children at school, but often she didn't understand things, or the lights or noises and smells were too much for her, and she would get overwhelmed and start screaming. And Beatrix would beat Millie over the head with the flat of her hand or with a book or other object to make her shut up. One day, Dana had told the social worker what Beatrix did to Millie, and after that, she and Cale had been moved again.

It occurred to Dana that whatever Ivor Pilgrennon had done to Jananin Blake, Ivor Pilgrennon was not like Beatrix. He was trying his best.

Peter picked up a chair and hoisted it up over his head. "Peter, no!" Ivor held up his hands.

"Peter, stop it!" Dana said.

Peter turned to her, his face distorted with emotion. He tried to force his horrible thoughts into Dana, but she pushed him out in the same way Cale did to her whenever he didn't want her there.

"Peter, don't throw that chair at me, because it will hurt me," Dana continued. "Why are you doing this?"

Peter dropped the chair on the floor. He raised his fists in front of his forehead and hunched his shoulders, and let out a long cry of despair.

Ivor stood motionless, watching Dana. Dana looked from Peter to him, and back again.

"Peter, can you tell me, can you *think* to me, why you

hurt, so I can understand?"

Peter took his hands away from his face. He started to cry in big, vocal sobs. Tears streaming down his face, he took a step towards the fish tank and pointed through the glass, to where a small fish floated upside-down on the surface.

"Oh, Peter," said Ivor, laying his hand on the boy's shoulder. "I don't think those little ones live very long. You take care of them so well, but it just *happens* sometimes."

-11-

"**H**E'S asleep, now," said Ivor, through the door to the computer room where Dana was sitting. "Come and sit down, talk to me for a minute."

Dana came back into the bedroom. He sat in the armchair and Dana sat uneasily on a footstool.

"He always sleeps well after every one of his outbursts." Ivor shook his head, flashing a humourless smile. "At my age, I can only *dream* of sleeping that well."

After Dana said nothing for several minutes, he ventured, "You like flowers, don't you, Dana?" He held out a small book to her: *The Collins Gem Guide of Wild Flowers*.

"I like plants," Dana said as she took the book. "I like their Latin names."

"Everything has a Latin name. Not just plants. You and I for example. We're called humans, or Men, but our proper name is *Homo sapiens*. It means 'knowing man'." He leaned back on the chair and folded his arms. "Thing is, more I know, the more I realise there is that I don't know. Nobody can ever know everything."

"I know everything," said Dana. "I'm not supposed to. The computers tell me."

Ivor leaned forward, resting his forearms on his knees. "Well, Peter is autistic, like you are, but he also has something called ADHD. Attention Deficit Hyperactivity Disorder. He did have some medicine that was helping him with it, but it ran out a few months ago. He was doing okay. I was hoping he was getting better as he got older." He put his hands over his face, rubbing his palms against his eyelids. "I worry about the future for Peter and Alpha. And about you and your brother. I'm truly sorry you didn't find an adoptive family."

"Cale and I are all right, for now." Dana thought of Pauline and Graeme, and Duncan. She liked them, but the other families she and Cale had been with had never lasted.

Ivor took a lidded metal box from a shelf. A flower pattern had once been painted on it, but it was so old and bashed about it was hard to see. He opened the box and took out a key. "You'd better have this. It's the only spare key I've got to the computer room, so be careful you don't lose it, and to lock the door when you've finished so Peter doesn't go in there."

Dana put the key into her pocket with the fuses. As she sat there looking at Ivor, she noticed again the scratch marks on his arms, a bruise on the side of his jaw where Peter had head-butted him. "Can you get more medicine for Peter?"

"Potentially, but it would be difficult. I'd have to go to Lewis. It would take a lot of planning, and there's a risk involved. If I were to get caught, I'd probably go to prison. Not for very long, but Peter and Alpha have nobody else. They would get taken into care. Alpha would likely end up in an institution, and Peter, I don't know. Maybe he would get fostered like you, maybe not. I don't think he'd like it, either way."

Dana thought again of Beatrix, how she used to raise her hand high over her head, to put in as much force as possible when she hit.

"Do you think if I went with you, it would help? I can talk to lots of things. Traffic lights and cameras, not just computers. If you tell me what you need to do, I'll see if I can do it."

Ivor smiled and nodded. "I'll have a think about how we can do it. It's kind of you to offer. Anyway, you wanted to use the computer. I'd better give you some peace and quiet." He hesitated for a moment, then cleared his throat. "I don't mind you looking at whatever you want on it, but please don't use it to contact anyone, to tell anyone where you are or about me. Do remember that if you want to leave at any time, you have only to ask. I say that for Peter and Alpha's sake, as well as my own."

"Okay," said Dana. She did her best to smile, but she wasn't very good at it.

Ivor smiled back. He put his hand on her shoulder and gave it a squeeze on his way out.

Before Dana did anything else on Ivor's computer, she got out Jananin's laptop and balanced it on her knee. Dana quickly changed all the registration data to her own name. She moved all of Jananin's files and disguised them as system software. She closed the computer and put it back in the bag.

Dana had meant to look up more about Jananin Blake on the Internet, but the computer was still open on the page she'd last been on. The code on that page reminded her of something, and now she realised what it was. It was like the game she often played with Duncan, *Pillage and Burn*.

Dana sat on the floor, back against the wall, and closed her eyes and concentrated. Different, yet familiar. It was the difference between looking at something in code and the same thing as graphics, or a program. With her eyes shut, she could see images and videos on computers more easily. But this wasn't a picture, and there was no screen to give her a prompt as to how it was meant to be interpreted. It was something much more complicated.

The riot of data suddenly took form. The floor transitioned into rock where she sat; the thunder of running water filled her ears. Bright sunlight made her squint.

This was a game, but it was the most detailed and realistic game Dana had ever seen. It was set in a desert landscape, but in front of her a waterfall ran from the top of a cliff into a narrow canyon many yards below, throwing up spray that made rainbow effects in the sun and flowing onwards as a large stream, or perhaps a small river.

Birds with high crests and long, upright tails flitted between hairy-trunked trees with many branches that ended in grass-like clumps. Tiny owls crept in and out of burrows in the sandy soil, scorpions and lizards basked on rocks in the sun, and hares loped. At Dana's feet, a tortoise peered up at her, its head partly retracted into its shell. Farther away, herds of antlered deer and sheep-like creatures with horns grazed on the scrub.

Some distance downstream, Dana noticed the figure of a tall, gaunt man, standing with his back to her and throwing stones down the canyon.

He had very dark skin but his hair was a blond mohawk, and he wore what appeared to be ordinary jeans and trainers. As she moved closer, she noticed a pattern of curling, thin white lines all over his back.

Dana had found this game online, so perhaps it was an online, multiplayer game. *Pillage and Burn* had an online MMO mode, but Pauline was very strict that Duncan and Dana were only allowed to play the offline version, and didn't allow Duncan to have an Internet connection in his bedroom. Bullies could come in the house and bully you that way, and strangers could interact with you online, she said.

"Hello," said Dana. "Are you a player, or an NPC?"

The man turned to her with a start. His patterned skin was very black, almost blue, in a way that wasn't exactly realistic, and the irises of his eyes were silver. "I'm a player. Where'd you get that skin?"

When Dana didn't answer, he said, "Why do you look like that?"

Dana looked down at herself. Everything seemed in order. She looked back at the man's curiously marked face. "Because it's in my genes?" Pauline always used to say that it was in Dana's genes if anyone other than

Pauline remarked that she shuffled when she walked.

"It looks too realistic to be your own mod. I didn't even realise you could create an avatar that looked like a child."

Dana realised what she'd done. She was projecting her everyday appearance onto her avatar in the game. In *Pillage and Burn*, you had to make an avatar from available choices, as she'd done with the dwarf wizard and Duncan had done to make his giantess warrior.

"I didn't see the loading screen where you create an avatar. I think the game just gave me a random one. How do I get another?"

"You get skins as rewards for completing difficult puzzles here." He pointed his thumb back at himself. "This is the Charon skin. You only get access to it for completing the Charon puzzle. And then you can apply it to your avatar — that's how you look here. I've only seen one other player with the Charon skin, but he doesn't come here any more."

"Did he die?" Dana asked.

"If you die in the game, you just get reset. He might have died in real life, though. Or maybe he just got a girlfriend." He narrowed his eyes. "I don't know where you got that one from. I've never seen that hairstyle or that outfit before, and I've definitely not seen a child avatar. Although I don't suppose many people would use it, I mean, it's unusual and it's well rendered, but it kind of looks like those creepy kids off *The Shining* and *The Exorcist* or whatever those horror films were called."

Dana decided not to say anything in response to this. "So, you're Charon, the Ferryman to the Underworld?" She imagined this character with his silver eyes and otherworldly tattoos, were he dressed in a hooded robe on a ferry, from the myth and not the sort that carried cars and passengers between Scotland and Lewis, would have a very different effect than it did with the incongruous outfit and hairstyle this player had paired it with.

"I guess so, since I completed the puzzle to reach his boat."

"Says on your computer your name's Eric Cartwright."

Charon the Ferryman's face fell. "You hacked me? How'd you do that?"

"My name's Epsilon," said Dana, not wanting to tell him her real name. "Can you tell me more about this game? Is it about Cerberus, the three-headed dog?"

Eric folded his arms and leaned back on his heels. "If you're such a great hacker, why can't you find it out yourself?"

"Please will you play with me?" Dana looked down at the flashing patterns of sunlight on the shallow water as it tore over the boulders that strewed its bed. "I used to play *Pillage and Burn* with my foster brother, but he's not here now."

"I used to play *Pillage and Burn*," said Eric, "before I found this game. It's mint! It's a sandbox game. The whole thing is, like, an Easter Egg, because you don't have to pay for it, and you can hack into it, and there are a couple of online forums, but other than that nobody much is aware of it. It might be a beta test that's leaked, of something that hasn't been released yet."

Dana spotted something moving in the scrub. A large, dun-coloured cat was slinking nearby. She pointed to the cat and said to Eric, "If you want to kill it, I'll heal you."

"That's just a puma," said Eric. "This isn't really the sort of game where you kill things. The first time I got into it, I tried to kill the animals to see if you could get XP, or if you could eat them and learn cooking skills. You can hit them but they don't die. They usually just run away. I chucked a tortoise down the gorge onto the rocks, and it just lay there on its back with its legs moving until I logged out." Eric watched the puma for a moment. "And besides, I like cats."

"Can you show me what you can do in this game, then, please?"

"Oh, all right, but only if you show me how to get that skin in return."

"I thought you said this skin doesn't look very nice."

"It doesn't, but I haven't got it and I don't know anyone else who has." Eric grinned, and the effect with his strange haircut on the patterns on his face and his unnatural eye colour was rather disturbing. "And *they* won't know where I got it from."

"If this is the Styx, do we have to cross it?

"Look, I only navigated the Styx once, and I only really managed it through chance. And the program adapts. It changes when someone solves the puzzle to make it more difficult. I've not been able to get in since. The one time I did get to Cerberus, it threw me in the river and I died."

"Oh. Right." Dana turned to look up towards the source of the water, where it gushed from a hole halfway up a rockface.

Eric, or Charon, or whoever he was, turned and set off over the rocks at a great striding pace. "We have to climb up to where the water comes out and take Charon's ferry."

Dana followed his route among the boulders and pillars and great slabs around the serpentine path the river had carved for itself. The water glistened like mercury where sunlight penetrated the deep shade at the bottom of the gully. Underneath the mirage, Dana sensed the mass of impenetrable code she had seen at the gateway. Now she could assign fragments of code that had not meant anything to phenomena in the creation she was seeing.

A complex subroutine controlled the brown dragonflies that flitted over the water, gleaming like brass in the sun. The water was a repeating loop, and throughout the scenario were the coordinates that coded for the rocks and solid landscape and the colours and textures they were painted with.

Eric stopped beside the crevasse. Dana came to his side and peered down. The luxuriant fronds of a fern hung still and dense from a crevice in the rock, a shaft of sunlight falling across the tips and casting a refraction pattern of rainbow hues into the mist rising from the waterfall.

Eric pointed up at where the water thundered out of the cliff. "We can't climb up there. The only way up to the mouth of the Styx is on the other side." He moved his hand to point at some stumpy cycads growing on either side of a path. "The last time I completed this puzzle, there was a tree growing right here." Eric indicated a mangled stump at his feet. "The program's changed." He looked back over his shoulder, then set off back down the path.

"Where are you going?"

"To find a tree. I crossed it before by felling a tree and using it as a bridge."

"Wait. There's an easier way." Dana turned back to the gap. The fissure was about six yards across. There was no way any normal person could jump such a distance in real life, but Dana could find in the programming a constant that determined the gravitational force. She ran two steps to the edge and jumped, and at the critical point as she launched herself, she changed the constant from 1 to 0.25. The cleft and its glittering water flew beneath her. She changed the constant back to 1 as she landed. Dana looked back to where Eric stood, open-mouthed on the other side.

"Come on!"

"How did you do that?"

"Just jump and I'll fix it for you!"

Eric hesitated before taking a run-up and leaping like an athlete. Dana changed the gravity again and he sailed through the air like a flying theatre actor on a wire. He stumbled on landing, falling down on his knee as Dana reset the gravity. He put one fist on the ground, muscles in his thick shoulder bunching, and faced Dana. "What the hell?"

"I'm a, like what you said, a hacker." Dana shrugged.

The track steepened. Soon Eric was climbing above her and she was grasping rocks loose with moss. Dana slipped and smashed her knee painfully against the stone.

"Wait a minute," she gasped.

"What?"

"I'll be alright in a minute." Dana rubbed her knee.

"When I said I'd group with you, I didn't realise you were going to RP all the way."

The noise of the water tumbling to earth just a few feet away near deafened her. She could feel the current in the air the passage of the water created, the vapour settling on her skin.

Dana wondered if she might cheat at climbing by turning off the gravity completely and floating up the rockface. Then she supposed the whole thing might disintegrate and end up drifting skywards in tumbling boulders and clods of moss. Besides, when she cheated at games with Duncan, it always made them less fun in the long run.

"Okay." She resumed the climb.

"Nearly there," said Eric not long later.

Dana found she could only understand this world, ascribe code to effects, when she could see it. Otherwise, it was like trying to hear a single voice drowned out in a cacophony of others. She wondered how Eric navigated this world in the virtual way whoever had created it had intended it to be navigated — perhaps VR imaging equipment filled his eyes and hands. There were newer and more innovative ways of playing games than the handheld controllers Duncan used.

Eric clambered up through the gap where the water

made its egress. He straddled the gushing stream to face her. "Don't stand in the water. It comes out so fast it'll blast you off the cliff. I must've died about six times trying to get up here."

Dana reached up for the ledge. It was awkward: she couldn't put her foot up without grabbing on to something, and she couldn't grab anything without leaning over the water.

Eric laughed, but it wasn't an unkind laugh, so Dana laughed too.

As she was concentrating, trying to understand the subroutine for the water and how she might change it to make this easier, Eric made a grab for her hand.

"Careful!"

Dana slipped and her foot ended up in the water. The force threw her leg back. She lost her grip on Eric. In confusion she fell, the warm sun in the blue sky and the waterfall and the desert turning over. Then, just as she'd pushed her way into the program, the code pushed her back out, and she was sitting on the floor in the computer room, cold and dark and uncomfortable.

She locked the door when she left the room, and put the key safely back in her pocket. The door to Peter's bedroom stood open. He slept on the bed, one arm dangling over the side.

It was almost as strange being here as it was playing a game, but somehow it was starting to feel normal.

She found Ivor in the kitchen. He had already tidied up most of the things Peter had broken. Alpha was sitting at the chess table, staring into space.

"Ah, there you are. Do you want to come with me to check the lobster traps? Let's hope we've caught one, otherwise there'll just be potatoes and salad for dinner."

Outside, it was windy and already quite dark. Ivor brought a torch and Dana stood beside him and shone it where he directed her to as he pulled in the lines attached to the baskets. The first two came up empty, but when he pulled in the third, he exclaimed, "Aha!"

He returned the empty baskets to the sea with overarm throws. Dana held the torch on the basket so he could reach in and grab the lobster by the rear part of its carapace.

"But it's blue," said Dana. "The one yesterday was red."

"They don't turn red until you cook them," Ivor explained. "Can you hold the bag open so I can put it in? Mind it doesn't pinch you!"

He held out a folded cloth bag in his other hand. Dana opened it, trying to keep the torch still as he put the lobster inside. Ivor threw the last trap back, and he and Dana made their way back to the door into the island, carrying their lobster.

In the kitchen, Ivor set some pans of water to boil. "What were you doing in the computer room? I did look in on you, but your eyes were shut and I don't think you heard me. You looked a bit dissociated."

"I was playing an online game," said Dana. "I think when other people play the game, they maybe use a VR headset, or something like that. But when I play games, I just need to concentrate hard enough, and I can go into them. I forget where I really am, and it's like the game is real instead."

Ivor laughed. "When I was young, we had games. They were nowhere near as complicated as what you have now. When I was very young, I remember playing *Pac Man* and *Space Invaders* in an arcade. Then when I was an older boy, we had cartridge games with controllers that plug into the television. Platform games like *Sonic the Hedgehog* and *Super Mario*."

"This one is in a desert, and it's about Greek mythology. It's a sandbox game, and you don't kill things, but there are puzzles to solve."

Ivor looked at her intently. "About Greek mythology?"

Adults were not usually interested in games. If Dana

spoke to Pauline about games, she said they were a load of violent rubbish, and Graeme would just politely say he was too old for that sort of thing.

"There is the river Styx, and another player said he had solved the Charon puzzle, and I think it led him to Cerberus, the three-headed dog."

"Did you see Cerberus?"

"No, I was trying to solve a climbing puzzle with the other player to get to it, but I made a mistake and fell from a waterfall and died in the game."

"That sounds exciting," said Ivor. "Do you think you will play it again?"

"Yes. The graphics in it were really good. And games that are hard and where you die sometimes are more fun, really. I can cheat at Duncan's games, but really it makes it not fun any more when I do it too much. You don't mind if I play games online? It's just Pauline doesn't let me. She says there might be strangers, or bullies."

Ivor put the potatoes into a pan of boiling water. "I can see Pauline's concern, but I think, given the abilities you have, and your individual level of maturity, it's probably best for you to learn as soon as possible how to protect yourself from that sort of thing. Remember what I said about not giving away any details about yourself, or me, and if somebody is bothering you online or says anything that sounds off or inappropriate, let me know and we'll work out how to deal with it together. If playing online games is what you enjoy, there's nothing wrong with that."

He cautiously opened the bag on the scratched-up kitchen worktop. When he held the lobster over the steam it became lively, writhing its legs and snapping its pincers. He thrust it into the pan and slammed the lid down on top of it.

Something in Dana's expression must have given away the horror she felt at seeing this. Ivor said in haste, "I'm so sorry I forgot to warn you about that. Lobsters have quite simple nervous systems, more like insects than mammals or even fish. It's best to just put them in as fast as possible so it's over quickly for them."

The potatoes, the salad, and the lobster were set out on the concrete table, and Ivor went to rouse Peter from his sleep. When he came and sat down at the table, he looked exhausted. Dana took her seat on one of the metal folding chairs, but it was badly battered and it wobbled, refusing to stand properly with all four feet on the floor.

Ivor came back with the hammer, which he must have hidden somewhere else to stop Peter getting it during his rage. He broke up the lobster and divided the meat between the four of them. "Do you want the shell and the legs to pick at, Peter?"

"Too tired," Peter replied.

"Eat your dinner, Alpha." Ivor set Alpha's plate in front of her. Dana watched her eating mechanically. Alpha didn't think for herself. She only did what Ivor told her to.

Dana looked at the steaming red shell of the lobster and the meat on her plate, and thought of how it had looked before Ivor put it in the pan. But she was hungry, and the taste and texture of the lobster meat were good, and she supposed the meat and fish that came from the supermarket at Pauline and Graeme's house must have been killed somehow before it ended up in a packet. It didn't matter so much when she thought of it like that.

After dinner, Dana helped Ivor wash the pots and tidy up. He told Alpha to come into the kitchen, where she sat on a floor bolster and stared in front of her, and Peter went back to bed of his own choice.

"I've had a look at the weather forecast." Ivor washed a pan and set it to drain. "The tides and the weather should be conducive to going to Lewis in a few days, if you're still up for coming with me to get some medicine for Peter. We'll have to get some other supplies too: some more books to read, and some food."

"Okay," said Dana.

"It'll take some planning, and I've not worked out all the details yet, but we'll go through it the day before."

He washed the cutlery and set that down. "And perhaps don't talk to Peter about your game. Unfortunately he can't interface to computers like you can. He tries to, but they agitate him, and he breaks them. I've tried various things to help, but nothing's worked yet. That's why I made him that Viking helmet, because he likes Vikings, and to screen him from signals and keep his own signal contained. I think if you told him about games online, he would want to be able to play them, and then he'd be upset when he couldn't."

-12-

DANA went back to the computer room after dinner to see if Eric was still playing the Cerberus game. He was, and it appeared he'd died in it again, because he was back where they'd started.

"I'm glad you came back, actually," he said. "I'm starting to wonder if it's getting harder because it's supposed to be multiplayer."

"Want to try again?" Dana offered.

They set off up the cliff once more. This time when they reached the waterfall, Dana was more careful, and managed to climb up with Eric's help without being swept away by the water.

The river ran through a deep channel in the rock, so straight it could not be natural. Dana walked with a foot on either side of it, the tunnel not wide enough to permit walking on one side or the other.

She reached out with both arms to touch the wet walls with her fingertips. If not for the sunlight illuminating the mouth of the Styx and the tropical smell of lush vegetation penetrating the cave, this place could be Roareim.

The cave opened out to a platform either side of the water. There was no light, and Dana could see nothing of what lay inside. In front of her, she heard Eric go off to the left, and stepped after him.

"What are you doing?"

"There's a switch round here." Eric shuffled against the wall. Beneath his fingers, something glowed. The light pivoted out of the rock. "There are six of them. Three on this side and three on the other." He waved his hand. "Find them and turn them on."

Dana hopped over the river. Once the first lights were found and offered some illumination, it was easier to find the others. She could make out the cavern now: towards the back a semicircle carved from the stone held a reservoir of deep water, from which the channel she and Eric had followed up ran. Where the channel began it split in two, rejoining again to form a large rhombus island. There were no ledges on the sides of the reservoir by which to pass further up the course of the river.

"You see the markings on them?"

Dana turned the third light carefully. It was mounted on gimbals in the rock. Many graduations in the brass mount showed different positions the light could be set. Eric finished rotating the lights on his side.

"Do we have to swim through it?"

"No, you can't swim in this world, you just sink. And if your head's under for more than a minute, you die. There's a sequence of settings for the lights. It took me a long time to find them and work out what they were for. They're in a separate puzzle to this." He jumped over the water to join her and began moving between the lights, adjusting each. "If they are all set right, the next puzzle will be revealed."

Beams of light began to converge in the air. Patterns took form on the flat stone lozenge in between the channels of water. When Eric had adjusted the final light, he stepped over the channel onto the stone and knelt on one end of it. Dana knelt facing him on the opposite end.

Scratched into the centre of the stone lozenge was a nine-by-nine grid. The lights on the wall cast a coloured spot in each square.

"The puzzle's evolving," Eric muttered. "The other times I've solved this, all the lights were the same colour."

"How did you solve it?"

"You have to touch the squares to turn the lights off or on. Only when you touch a square, it affects the state of the other squares next to it." He reached out with his long, dark finger and touched a red light. The lights in the four squares directly next to it changed colour, whereas the red light Eric had touched disappeared. Randomly he touched another square to his right, a blue one, and all the squares diagonal to it changed, right to the sides of the board.

"Oh!" Dana cried excitedly, remembering playing chess with Ivor on Roareim. "It's like chess! Look, that's like a bishop!" She reached for a light of the third colour — green. When her finger touched the stone, the three squares directly and diagonally in front changed, the red and blue ones becoming green, the green one disappearing. Eric touched a green light, but the three squares it affected this time were below it from Dana's perspective. The puzzle must be able to detect the direction from which it was touched.

"That one's sort of a pawn. And I suppose the red one is like a king."

"Kings do diagonals as well. I suppose we must just have to keep chasing them round until they all go out. It's more like draughts than chess."

"There must be a quicker way." Dana leaned forward on her knees over the board. "I wonder if it will let you make two moves at once?"

She touched a green square and a red square one up and two to the right of the green one. The affected squares all changed to either red or green accordingly, but the red one where the two moves intersected, on the left of the red and diagonally right of the green, became blue.

"There are three colours," she said, "and each one makes a different pattern. If you touch two at once, and they overlap, it changes to the colour the two you touch aren't. So what happens if you touch three at once and they all affect the same square?"

"It'd be a paradox." Eric shifted off his knees onto

the sides of his legs, bending his feet under him. "It'd probably just go blank."

They pressed a few more squares, and ascertained that Eric's presumption was correct. If a square was told simultaneously to be two colours, it would be the third colour. If it was told simultaneously to be three colours, it would go blank.

"What if the square is already blank?" Dana hovered her hand over the grid, deliberating which square to choose. Their experimentation had caused some of the lights to turn off. Dead in the centre square, no light shone.

"There has to be a change of state every time. So if it's already off, it can't be off, and if it's being told three times to be three different things, it can't possibly be any of them." Her hand hung still over the square as she remembered an experiment that had once been demonstrated to her by taping bits of coloured tissue paper over three torches and shining the light in the same place.

Dana pointed out a green light directly above the blank square. "See the green light? Put your finger over it, but don't touch it until I say."

On the direct left of the square was a red light, and Dana held her left index finger over this. A knight's move right and down of it was a blue light. If these three colours were touched, the puzzle would try to make the centre square be red, green, and blue all at once.

"It's starting to get more like Twister than draughts or chess," complained Eric.

"One, two, three, go."

Dana and Eric touched the board simultaneously. Multiple lights around the grid changed colour, but a white light appeared in the centre square.

"White?" said Eric. "What's white?"

They took their fingers away from the board and, for a few seconds, neither said anything.

"It's the queen," Dana realised, and impulsively she touched it. White lights spread outward across the board, then all the lights went out.

A concussion shook the floor, the tremor giving the river a brief appearance of boiling, and the board cracked under Dana's finger. She pulled her hand away as the rhombus split down its width, straight as a ruler. Eric seized her arm as the floor tilted up, tipping both of them towards the deep water.

They fell forward together into the gap revealed by the broken rhombus. Dana's feet landed on something that lurched up to meet them and moved with an unbalancing swaying motion. She sat down hard on a wooden plank and twisted to look over her shoulder, recognising the prow of a boat. It slipped into the water with a jolt and a bow wave that spread over the underground pool.

They sat facing each other as the rocking of the boat slowed. "It's Charon's ferry," Dana realised.

Eric took hold of a long pole attached to the side of the boat. He sank the end of it deep into the water and pushed against the ground. The boat moved upstream, into the rocky arch of the pathless cave.

Dana leaned forward over the stem of the boat as they advanced, peering down into water black and reflective as obsidian. She strained her eyes to descry what might lie below its surface, but all she saw was the greyish boards of the ferry and her own face. As they slid further into the deep river, the light from the room behind dimmed until Dana could no longer see the surface of the water or her own hands on the rim of the boat.

The light diminished to a tiny golden half-moon far behind. Leaning forward trying to make out what lay ahead, Dana just had time to bring her hands before her face as the keel struck something with a jerk and a scrape, and she pitched forward over the bow and her hand hit rock. The boat began to slide back downstream, and she clutched at its stem to stop herself from going overboard in its wake.

"Are you still aboard?" Eric called in the dark.

"Yes," said Dana. "I think the river bends."

Eric pushed the boat a little to the left. "The current still comes from straight ahead. It's getting stronger as well." The boat bumped against the wall and scraped to the left as Eric pushed back.

"Can you keep it still?"

Eric gave the pole another shove. "Not really."

Dana leaned over the prow and reached down to the surface of the water. A foot or so from the rim of the boat, the wall sloped inwards. The drift of the boat pulled her hand away. She withdrew quickly in case Eric decided to push the boat into the rock again. "The ceiling's lower. Like a bridge. The boat won't fit under it."

"Why is the water flowing faster?" Eric muttered, moving about in the boat. Dana heard the plop of the pole entering the water, and the muffled thud of it striking rock below. "The water close to the wall is shallow! That's why the water flows faster."

"How shallow?"

"Try getting out of the boat," Eric suggested.

"Are you sure?"

"Just try it. Unless either of us have another idea, we're stuck here. If you die we'll just have to start again."

Dana wondered if time passed here at the same rate as it did back in Roareim. Was Ivor sitting, reading a book in the kitchen, or had he gone to bed? The boat tilted as she straddled its side. "Don't run me over with it."

The water was icy cold. Once her foot was in she tried to lower herself slowly, but the boat began to tilt at an alarming angle and she tipped off. Her head went under the water, and inside the program a timer started counting down from sixty. Then her feet found the floor. She gasped as the cold and pressure of the water tightened around her chest. "It's not deep!" she called to Eric in a thin voice.

"Here, take the pole." The pole hit Dana over the head before she managed to get hold of it. Eric got her to hold on to the front of the boat while he jumped off, landing in the water with a splash. They turned the boat over so the sides were in the water and the keel was up, supported on the air trapped inside it.

Dana felt the boat sink slightly as Eric leaned down hard on it. "Now, try to push it underneath!"

They both leaned on the boat and pushed against the lip in the rock where the ceiling lowered. "We don't know how long the roof is going to be this low," Dana said, struggling against the boat.

"Once it's in the rock'll hold it there."

The prow of the boat began to slide into the hole, its underside grating on the roof. Then Dana lost her grip and it shot up like a cork. Eric caught it before it flew off downstream and pulled him off the shallow ledge.

"C'mon, let's try again," he said.

This time he leaned across the rear of the boat until it was wedged in three quarters of the way. "Now, go under it and push forwards."

Dana gave him back the ferryman's pole and ducked under the side of the boat. She came up with her head in the airspace trapped beneath it. She at once went forward and set her hands against the wood. The boat scraped. Eric came up behind her. He leaned forward and put an arm either side of Dana, and together they pushed onward.

Pushing the boat through the tunnel went on interminably. Dana started to worry that the ceiling would wear a hole in the bottom of the boat so that it wouldn't work if they ever got out of this constriction in the passage of the Styx.

Then she felt a hand grab her ankle.

"There's someone in the water!"

"Just keep pushing!" Eric gave the boat a hard shove, and it rasped along the stone ceiling.

The hand on Dana's leg gripped tightly, pulling, and now the person in the water had got hold of her other ankle. "Someone in the water is trying to pull me under and drown me!"

A third hand grabbed hold of Dana's left knee. Eric backed up and slammed into the front of the boat. The planks shrieked, the boat popped up, and Dana caught sight of a roiling surface in an eerie green light, before the hands pulled her legs from under her. The timer began to count down from sixty again, and she was being dragged upstream into deeper water. She called for Eric and the sound came out as an elephant noise and a stream of bubbles.

Another hand grabbed her by the arm, just above the elbow, wrenching her back. As her head came above the surface she realised it was Eric. He'd flipped the boat back over and he flung her into it. He staggered in the water, arms flailing, struggling to keep upright. Dana looked down at her legs and screamed, for the things that had grabbed her underwater were not people as she'd assumed, and they were still hanging on grimly.

They clung to her with the thumbs and fingers of human hands, but where the wrist should have been the skin merged seamlessly into slimy scales and gills on either side, turning into the long, writhing bodies of subterranean fish. The fish bodies thrashed and flapped violently, beating her with their thorny tails. Dana prised apart the fingers of the one on her knee. The fish-hand fell into the boat and started kippering about, groping manically.

Eric heaved himself up on the side of the boat. Where his feet rose, fish tails thrashed. The boat tilted and Dana threw herself hard against the opposite side as water with voracious fish-hands swimming in it spilled over the side. Eric lurched into the boat, throwing it right again, and it floated with mere inches of its walls above the water. Dana began bailing with her hands as the boat ran back against the tunnel entrance. She threw away the fish-hands. Eric too began to bail, planing the water over the sides. Gradually, they floated higher. Eric resumed poling the boat upstream while Dana continued to scoop up the water.

A greenish glow lit the Styx, glinting upon razor-sharp edges on the mountains at its banks. Dana assumed they were unscaleable, that any player who tried to scramble up them would die an unpleasant death of lacerations. Although she craned her neck, all she could see above was a distant black ceiling, hung with stalactites, which joined to the bank to form pillars in places. The light emanated from a phosphorescent mist overhanging the water. The deep-throated gurgle of the river's flow and the steady drip-drip from the stalactites were the only sounds she heard, save for the occasional echoing subterranean groan, as if tectonic plates moved against one another.

Eric spoke less as they headed farther upstream, concentrating on using the pole to push against the current.

They passed a place were two rounded, polished stones banded with minerals protruded from the water close to each bank, like gateposts on either side of an entrance.

"Hold on," said Eric.

"What?"

"This is the place where I always die."

The water beneath the boat swelled into a tidal wave of foam. The boat reared into the air, its stern pitching down. Eric poled hard towards the bank, trying to keep the boat centred on the wave, but it spun, torn by opposing currents. The wave broke upon both shores, sending the boat drifting back downstream. A great swell sloshed over everything, and Dana was down in the water, the timer starting again and the fish hands latching upon her legs and arms.

And then she was back in the computer room on Roareim, her heart pounding in her chest.

Dana stood up and felt for the computer to find what time it was: ten past eleven. She came out of the room to find the bedroom beyond it dimly lit, and Ivor sprawled across the bed, asleep. He was snoring slightly, and he reminded Dana of a couple of times when Graeme, after a demanding day at his work, had fallen asleep in front of the television. She crept out the door and went back to her bedroom.

-13-

ERIC was not online for the next two days. Dana wondered if he was busy with something else, or if he just happened not to be on at the times when she was available.

She considered playing solo and retrying the Styx alone, but she didn't like the dark or the memory of those hands with fish tails and how it felt to be grabbed by them.

Instead, she explored the desert, which so far as she could tell went on forever. She found a cave with a simple puzzle of arranging stones in a pattern, which she solved easily, and for this she received a furry puma-skin gilet to wear in the game.

She spent a great deal of time observing the wildlife, marvelling at the intricate detail programmed into it and the realistic rendering. The puma followed the herds of sheep and deer, occasionally stalking and taking down a weak or young one. Birds picked lizards from rocks; hawks hunted hares. One time, Dana found a huge lizard with black and orange mottled skin, and out of curiosity had picked it up and tried to pet it, and it had bitten her. Its venomous bite made her feel ill and dizzy, and the game became blurry until she logged out and back in again.

Back in reality, her time was taken up with the routine on the island, and with helping Ivor work out a plan to go to the mainland to get medicine for Peter. Much of this involved Ivor asking her if she had experience of particular signals she might have come across in shops, or banks, or doctors' surgeries, and if she could interfere with them.

"How are we going to Lewis?" Dana asked him one morning, sitting in the kitchen while he wrote in a spiral-bound notebook on the chess table and Alpha stared into space from one of the floor cushions.

"In a boat." Ivor lowered his voice to a forcedly sinister tone. "Under cover of darkness."

"Is there a boat here?"

"I haven't got round to showing you the submarine bay yet, have I?"

"We're going to Lewis on a submarine?"

"Sadly, the military seem to have taken their submarine with them when they left, unless they scuttled it and it's lying on the bottom somewhere. You'll have to make do with an ordinary motorboat."

Fortunately, Peter didn't have another meltdown in the days before they left. He kept his helmet on and he read a lot of books, and he talked to Dana and Ivor about fish and Vikings.

The evening before the day arrived, and the air was very still. The sun set over the sea, leaving a pinkish glow that lit up a fine cirrus tracery in the western sky.

"Red sky at night, Shepherd's delight," said Ivor. He was resetting the rabbit traps, and when he concentrated, he drew his eyebrows down and jutted his bottom lip up and out, which somehow accentuated the size and sharp angle of his nose.

"Shepherd's *pie*," said Peter, who had been running around the beacon mast on the grass.

"It's a long time since we had shepherd's pie," said Ivor. "But we can see about getting the ingredients to make one when we're out tomorrow. Peter, come away from the edge."

"Can I come to Lewis tomorrow, Ivor?" Peter asked.

"We'll see. You have to be on your best behaviour if you do come."

Dana went to bed knowing she'd have to get up early in the morning, but it didn't make it any easier to open her eyes when Ivor came and shook her shoulder to wake her, and the excitement of going on a trip she'd helped to plan didn't make getting out of bed into the cold air or standing on the concrete floor any less unpleasant.

When Dana was dressed, she found Ivor with Peter in the kitchen. Peter was also dressed and wearing his helmet, and whining. He hung from Ivor's belt with his knees bent as though trying to pull the man's trousers down. Ivor ignored Peter, scraping food from a pan into a plastic box. Alpha sat in front of the chess table. The chessmen had been cleared away and a radio stood on the board, a lead running from it up into the concrete of the ceiling.

"Peter, *peter out.*" Ivor glanced to Dana. "We'll eat on the way." He put the lid on the box and slid it into a bag lying on the bench. He put on his spectacles and slapped his pockets with his hands. "Right, keys, wallet." He checked his waistcoat pocket again, pulled on his RAF jacket, and hoisted the bag onto his shoulder. He put a plate down in front of Alpha and pressed a button on the radio. A whirr, and a recording of Ivor's voice said, "Alpha, eat your food."

Alpha picked up her fork and started to eat the plate of potatoes and seagull.

"That works, then. Peter, stop doing that. What have I told you?"

"That I need to be on my best behaviour." Peter followed this with a wheedling noise and a shove at Ivor.

"Don't whinge, do as you're told, and if you take your helmet off, I shall never take you anywhere, ever again," he admonished the boy.

Peter immediately let go of Ivor and went to put his boots on. Dana found her original boots, which had now dried out.

Ivor led the way out by another door near the entrance. This time there were no stairs, and the door led to a cold cave filled with the stink of the sea. In the darkness came the slap of water against rock. A click, and a beam of light illuminated the side of a boat, moored inside Roareim.

Ivor supported Dana by the arm while she climbed into the boat, which lurched in response to her weight and made her think of both the ferry in the game and the stolen one she'd come here on and lost, both of which had been smaller, but not by a good deal. Ivor handed up the torch to her. There were seats in the front of the boat, and a steering wheel like in a car. Ivor helped Peter into the boat before climbing into the driver's seat. "Dana, you come and sit up here."

Dana clambered forward and shone the torch in Ivor's face.

"On there, please." He pointed to the grubby, water-stained instruments on the boat's dashboard. "Peter, sit down and don't fidget."

Dana shone the torch on the controls as Ivor turned the ignition key. He backed the boat out into dark water that boiled at the stern with the engine's churning.

Dawn had not yet begun to lighten the horizon, stars gleaming still in the black sky. The wind roared and shook the boat. Even though it was bigger than the other boats Dana had known, it still felt small upon the vastness of the ocean, in the even greater vastness of the dark.

The lighthouse beam swung about the darkness, casting shifting shadows and highlights over the rocks and spray. Dana shivered, wondering why the savagery of the wind and the ocean had not consumed the islands and the stars many eons ago.

Ivor pushed a lever and the boat moved forward. He turned the steering wheel so as to leave Roareim and its nearby rocks a wide berth. Dana looked over her shoulder to see saw a flaring trail of creamy foam stretching away behind the stern. The water was like black glass. The light, when it came, engulfed her vision and gave strange form to the sea and the occupants of the boat.

They passed Eilean Mór on the north side. As they raced ahead of the light, a tiny cluster of lights became visible in the approaching bulk.

"Oh, look!"

"That's Aird Uig," said Ivor. "We can't go there because it's too small and we'd stand out." He gave the wheel a sudden turn and the boat banked right, sending an arc of water into the air behind them. Dana saw the lighthouse beam catch it and light it up like a city fountain. Peter shouted. She laughed as she clung to the seat. Ivor shot a grin at her, caught briefly in the passing of the light.

"Where are we going, then?"

"Stornoway. That's the biggest town on Lewis, and where we stand least chance of being remembered."

The dark cliffs grew closer, towering over the boat as it tore south along the coastline. A few miles later, sparse lights came into view on two rock promontories where the land opened to the sea. As Ivor steered the boat into the cove, Dana looked up at the cliffs, featureless in the dark and rising sheer from the water. The boat slowed and Dana shone the torch over the bow. Calm waves lapped a smooth incline of glistening wet sand.

Ivor steered the boat into the mouth of a small river until the keel slid and the propellers thudded in the silt, and switched off the engine.

"Right, high tide was about an hour ago. We'll be able to get the boat out on the next one." Ivor's face appeared, lit by an eerie green underlight cast up from his watch as he set it. "That gives us until about five this evening. Peter, there's water on that side." He took hold of Dana's hands as she climbed onto the side of the boat, dangling her over until her feet touched the wet ground below.

Dana took a step forward to stop her feet sinking in the mud. Shining the torch about, she noticed the indentations she had left were steadily fading into the sediment.

Ivor landed heavily in the mud, sending a film of it

splashing out in a three-foot radius. The splattered sand quickly merged into the whole. Peter moved forward with a slurping sound.

"Don't stand still too long." Ivor took hold of Dana's arm. "Peter, hold my other hand. I don't want to lose you in the dark."

Peter started up a high-pitched giggle as they set off up the beach.

"How are we going to get to Stornoway? Ivor, Ivor, Ivor, Ivor," went Peter.

"Ivor car hidden here. So long as no-one's found it and taken it away. In which case we may have to," Ivor cleared his throat emphatically, "borrow one."

Dana was breathing heavily by the time the wet sand slackened, and Ivor half dragged Peter, who was still giggling and saying, "Ivor fish," and "Ivor motorboat." At last she felt sparse, dry grass under her feet and the ground no longer gripped her ankles.

The wind ripped over the rise of the land, the ellipse of light Dana's torch cast bouncing ahead as Ivor pulled them into a run. The land began to fall away. Dana saw no lights among the dark hills. The ground became steeper and they slid down the loose surface.

The ground levelled and the torch illuminated a stony-floored dip in the landscape. Ivor stopped and released Dana's and Peter's hands. "Ah," he said. He reached over and guided the aperture of Dana's torch to show a place where the earth rose between two boulders. "Car's still here."

"I see no car." Dana stared in the direction he'd pointed the torch. Her voice hardly penetrated the noise of the wind.

Ivor strode forward. He knelt down and started grubbing about in the soil of the slope. There came the fibrous sound of grass roots tearing. He caught hold of something and the surface shifted, earth sliding from a rotting plastic sheet. The reflective facets of a car's rear lights gleamed in the torchlight. Ivor pulled the cover away, revealing a spare tyre mounted on the rear of the vehicle. It was an old car, possibly as old as Jananin's, and it issued no signal; the legend on the back of the bodywork said it was a Landrover Freelander.

Ivor toed some rocks away from behind the vehicle and flattened the cover down to one side, placing some of the stones on it.

"Dana, you sit in the front."

The car smelt musty and mould grew on the seat. Dana slammed the door, shutting out the noise of the wind. "Are we going to steal the medicine when we get to Stornoway?"

Ivor was stuffing something into his mouth. "No." He swallowed. "We're going to have to forge a prescription. Only I don't know what prescriptions look like these days." He reached inside the bag and tossed an object to Dana. "See what you make of that." He fumbled some potatoes and mushed-up seagull into her hands in the dark, and passed the container to Peter in the back seat.

The artefact unfolded to make a long, flat thing with a slot on what appeared to be the top and side. "What is it?"

"It's a printer. It operates by an IR signal called Bluetooth — I don't know if that's still in use now." Dana heard him slot the keys into the hole under the steering wheel. "This had better start first try, or the battery won't have enough juice."

He took a deep breath, and turned the key. The dials on the dashboard lit up with a thump and a dieselly clatter.

For a moment they waited, eating seagull meat with seaweed and boiled potatoes in the car in the dark, the engine idling. Ivor switched on the headlamps and put his hand on the gear lever. The car made a noise. Ivor put his knee down harder. The car began to slide backwards. He turned the wheel and rock scraped against one of the tyres. Ivor swore breathily, eliciting laughter from Peter.

The car eased forward and turned, headlamps shining on a track.

"Is this car broken?" Peter asked.

"I think it's more the driver that's broken," Ivor said. "Took me five attempts to pass my test. Lack of practice the last few years doesn't help either."

Dana said, "I drive rubbish, too. I crashed into a signpost, and it wasn't even my own car."

Ivor turned his head to her.

"Look at the road!"

As they crested the hill the first light of dawn appeared on the eastern horizon. Dana sensed a sudden, unfamiliar signal.

"Wait a minute!"

Ivor braked hard.

"There's something here." Dana opened the door and got out. Ivor's door slammed behind her as she went along the edge of the road, turning her head this way and that to locate the direction. It came from a metal rod planted vertically in the ground.

Shaking stiffly in the wind, it looked as brittle as a dead flower. Dana poked the small electronic device at the top of the stalk.

Behind her, Ivor said, "It's probably something for counting the traffic or monitoring the weather here."

"But it wasn't here before."

"Perhaps it was and you just didn't notice it. We don't have time for distractions, Dana. We have to keep the focus on what we've come here for." When Dana turned back to look at him, he was scanning the horizon, twisting the gold ring on his left hand again. She followed him to the car.

The track became a road as they headed due east into the sunrise. Ivor pulled the visor down.

Dana tried to imagine Ivor driving this road in a hurry, years ago, the car stuffed with whatever he could gather at that time, Peter and Alpha bundled into the back, Alpha probably a young child and Peter little more than a baby. That part of Ivor and Jananin's accounts did agree. Perhaps Jananin had been pursuing them when they concealed the car and acquired the boat; perhaps this very car had been the one Ivor escaped in when the Compton bomb had wreaked its destruction. Unless Jananin had lied and there hadn't been a Compton bomb. Had Ivor known about the hidden army base on Roareim before he set out, or had he discovered it in desperation?

Now what did he intend, having left his hiding place? Just medicine to help Peter? He'd said he wanted Dana to forge a prescription. Was this what Jananin had meant when she'd said that Pilgrennon wanted to use Dana's abilities? Dana had left the bag with Jananin's computer in on Roareim. Perhaps she ought to have taken the computer with her. Then if it turned out Ivor was doing something illegal, there would be a mobile phone signal and she would have been able to call Jananin and ask her what to do.

She studied Ivor's face as he drove. He didn't look like someone who was going to do something bad.

A man and woman with a boy walked at the side of the road. The man turned his head to stare at Ivor's car.

"I'm bored," Peter whinged, and kicked Ivor's seat. "Are we nearly at Stornoway yet?"

Ivor glanced over his shoulder, making the car swerve. "Has he got his seatbelt on?"

"Peter, put your seatbelt on," said Dana. She pulled the strap of hers and pointed to the clasp beside the seat.

Peter looked at the clasp and stuck his finger in it.

"Peter, stop mucking about and put it on. If I crash the car you're going to go through the windscreen without it."

"I won't," Peter said. "You're in the way."

"You'll make a tasteless jacket then. And stop kicking the back of the seat."

Peter started clicking the knob that locked the door up and down.

Ivor sighed. "Peter, what did I tell you before we came out?"

"That I must be on my best behaviour."

"Then *be on it*. I know it's a change in routine, and it's difficult for you, but I need you to concentrate and do better."

They passed the place where Dana had crashed the car two days ago. The car had been taken away, but it had left a bend in the pole, the sign leaning into the road. She didn't say anything of it to Ivor and Peter.

"Now, Dana, I want you to use GPS to find me a doctors' surgery this side of Stornorway."

"Okay," said Dana.

After a long silence, Ivor said, "Well, have you found one yet?"

"Yes." There was one at Achmore, near where she had stolen the car.

"All right, then. Can you direct me to it?"

Dana remembered the route and told it to him as she had read it from the map and from memory. It did not feel so fast and out of control when Ivor drove as when she'd driven the car, even though she could see from the speedometer it was faster.

Ivor found a place to park and pulled the car over, the wheels scraping on the kerb. "Let's get some books, first."

Dana looked up and down the street. It was 9:05 and the only person in sight was an old woman in a mac with a grotty piece of material tied over her head, shuffling along with her face bent over the ground.

They got out and made their way over to the bookshop, Ivor's shabby RAF jacket flapping in the wind. Inside, an elderly man sat behind the counter. He looked up and mumbled a hello as they entered, but he squinted from behind smeary glasses, and Dana suspected his eyesight wasn't very good. There weren't any other customers.

The books exerted a calming effect on Peter. He went around the shelves, scanning them meticulously for any book that interested him, grinning all the time. A few times he came back to Ivor to request he fetch him a book he couldn't reach.

Dana found a book about carnivorous plants and another about aeroplanes from World War II. The planes looked exciting, with their camouflage paint and spots like targets on the wings.

When Peter had all the books he could carry, Ivor led them back to the counter. "Can you do me a deal on these? Oh, and a bag of jelly beans." He indicated to the old-fashioned jars of sweets behind the seller.

The old man craned his head to Dana and Peter, smiling feebly at them. Peter stuck his tongue out, but the man didn't notice. With trembling hands, he measured the jelly beans into a paper bag with a scoop, and accepted the notes Ivor gave him. Peter bounced from foot to foot as they walked back to the car. Once inside, Peter took out a book — a fish encyclopedia — and immediately started to read.

"Peter, can you wait in the car for a few minutes and take care of the books for us?"

Without looking up, Peter nodded. Ivor reached over him to slip some jelly beans into the gutter of Peter's book.

"C'mon, Dana," Ivor said, closing the door.

Dana stepped out into the road. Ivor came around the car and took hold of her sleeve as they crossed. He offered her the paper bag. Dana chewed the bean and walked close to him. Some distance away, a man was walking with a dog. He raised his hand in acknowledgement, and Ivor raised his in return. The man must think Dana and Ivor looked *normal*, Dana thought. Perhaps he thought she was Ivor's daughter, that they were going for a walk and eating jelly beans together, like normal fathers and daughters do.

"Where's the surgery?"

"It's round the back of these." Dana waved at the buildings beside the road. They followed the path along behind the shops.

Where the path opened out, a few willow trees had been planted. A moss-covered wooden fence stood at the edge of a small valley with a stream at the bottom. There were benches and some swings and a roundabout.

"That's the medical centre, over there." Dana pointed to the low, rounded building made from dull stone as if to camouflage its modern design.

"Can you sense a network yet?"

Dana was picking up a faint wLAN signal. "Yes."

"Okay." Ivor paused to survey the surroundings. "Let's try to look like we're doing something normal."

Dana sat on a swing.

Ivor gave her a push. "We're playing on the swings and we're not up to no good." He caught the swing and pulled her up and back, speaking quietly as he did. "Somewhere on their system they'll have a form layout, probably in the format of a database file, for printing prescriptions. I want you to find that."

Dana concentrated on the signal as Ivor pushed her on the swing, seeking through the other computers connected to it for what she needed. Ivor gave her a forceful shove. The chains on the swing went almost horizontal. Dana laughed and shouted at him, "The signal's going funny!" She gripped the chains tightly, trying to look over her shoulder. "I'll go over the top and land on your head!"

"You can't go over the top!" He was shaking his head and laughing. "The physics of it don't work that way."

"I think I've found the prescription — form!" Dana shouted as he launched her into the air again.

"Good!" Ivor grabbed her by the waist as she came back down and pulled her up into the air until he was holding up the swing by the seat. Dana leaned forward to look down at him between her knees. He was grinning like a lunatic. "Now you need to — fill it in," and he pushed again, and she screamed as tarmac hurtled up to meet her, "in the appropriate fields with Peter's details."

"What's Peter's name?" Dana asked as she swung back.

"Just call him Peter Piper. Pilgrennon is too distinctive."

"Oh, and I suppose people aren't going to think it's odd that he's called Peter — Piper! — then? And what am I supposed to put in the address field? Down a hole on — Roareim! — Flannan Isles?"

"Pick a random address in a Lewis town."

Dana did so. "What's the prescription for?"

"We need 'Ritalin SR' 30 mg x 100."

"Hang on a minute, there's another database connected to that field." Dana steeled herself for the impact as she swung back and Ivor pushed her again. "It says, Ritalin, discontinued, recommend Conurone or similar."

Ivor had apparently forgotten to step back, and Dana hit him in the stomach. She rebounded off him and put her feet down to brake on the tarmac, like a duck landing on water. She twisted around on the swing. He was frowning and making a winded noise. Dana laughed at him.

"Conurone?" he mused. "That must be a new market name for some other drug. Oh well, get that instead then. Get the highest pack number."

"That's 500 mg, 30 pills." Dana selected the option. "It says here, Doctor's name. Do I just choose any?"

"Yes, that's okay."

Dana chose a doctor called Brooke. "I think that's all of the fields. What do I do now?"

"On the prescription document there should be an option to print. I don't want you to print it yet, but I want you to try to work out the signal it would make in order to print the prescription on the Bluetooth printer I gave you in the car."

"Okay, I've done it."

"Good." Ivor came around the swing frame and sat down on the other swing. The frame creaked and an alarming tremor ran through it. The swing Dana was sitting on lowered a few inches.

Dana stared at him, still laughing. "You're going to break it! It's meant to be for kids, not for huge big men!"

Ivor arched his eyebrows and offered her the jelly beans. "Now, don't send the signal, just remember it for now." He made idle circling motions, the swing chains groaning, as he tipped the rest of the jelly beans into his hand and palmed them to his mouth, jerking his head back.

He got off, making the frame jump, and headed towards the large bin marked *non medical* at the back of the building, crumpling the paper bag in his hand. Dana watched from the swing as he lifted the lid and peered inside. She saw him drop the screwed-up bag, but at the same time he snatched something up with his other hand and shoved it under his jacket.

He walked briskly back to the swings. "C'mon, Dana. Let's hope Peter hasn't started eating the upholstery."

As they walked, he put his hand on her shoulder and tucked her under his arm, as though they were normal people going about their business. Not like a girl who was on the news as a missing person and a man who had just stolen something from a bin behind a medical centre.

Peter hadn't eaten the upholstery, Dana observed as they went back to the car, although he had spat all over the window. "Where have you been?"

Ivor pulled a wad of green paper out from his RAF blazer and balanced it on the steering wheel. Black ink had been spilt over it and dried on. Ivor ripped off a few of the stained upper sheets. The wad that remained just had ink on the edge.

Dana opened out the printer and Ivor balanced it on his knee. He tore off one of the green sheets and inserted the edge into the printer. "Okay, Dana. I want you to send the signal you remembered to the printer." He pressed the switch on the side of it.

Dana found the printer's fluttering little Bluetooth presence and locked onto it. It started up with a noise that made her jump. The green paper began to inch through the slot and out the other side. She picked up the edge as it dropped out. The data all looked to be in the right boxes.

"Very good!" Ivor took the prescription. "Now all we need is the signature."

Dana was exasperated. "You should've said before!"

"Never fear," said Ivor. He found a Biro in the car door and scribbled illegibly on the line.

"Won't they notice?" said Dana.

"Probably not. One GP's signature is much like another's, and much the same state as everything else they write, which is why prescriptions are printed on a form and not handwritten."

Ivor started the car and pulled away. Soon after he turned down a street they found a pharmacist, and he pulled over.

They left Peter in the car again. In the pharmacist, Ivor picked up some razor blades and a pack of toilet rolls before putting the prescription down on the table and making some marks on the back with a pen, and signing it. Dana stood close to him and noticed that the signature he used, although elongated and not completely legible, was still recognisable as saying something like 'IvrSPilgrennon', and wondered whether to remind him. The pharmacist took it without noticing the signature.

"So this is your son and he's under eighteen?" she asked Ivor.

"Yes."

The woman tapped a computer keyboard. "He's not on the system. Just a minute while I put him on." She glanced at Dana and smiled. "Have you moved here recently?"

"Yes," said Dana truthfully. "Just this weekend."

The pharmacist finished with the computer. Some labels issued from a small printer. She went to the back of the shop and turned a rack of medication around until she located a particular slot, from which she took some identical boxes. "Has Peter taken these before?" she asked as she stuck a label on a box.

"No, he's just had Ritalin before," said Ivor.

"Ritalin? I thought that was phased out a while back. I suppose they must still use it in some places? Normally they recommend one tablet with breakfast and another with a midday meal, but if you find he has trouble sleeping, just stick with the one in the morning." She finished putting the labels on and stood the boxes in a pile in front of Ivor. "Did you want anything else?"

"Packet of aspirins and some children's paracetamol syrup," said Ivor. "Oh, and a bottle of water." He indicated the refrigerated shelf at the side of the shop.

The pharmacist fetched the items, scanned them over a barcode reader, and put them with the heap of boxes. "That's twelve pounds twenty, then."

Ivor fished his wallet out of his trouser pocket. His expression suddenly changed when he opened it.

"Everything all right?" the pharmacist asked.

"Er, yes." Ivor took out a card and stuck it in a slot at the top of a keypad on the counter. When the woman looked down at her computer, Ivor looked at Dana, widened his eyes, and pointed at the card. She watched the device, not understanding. It was transmitting a signal. It beeped.

"Oh, hang on a minute. It reckons it's expired," the pharmacist said. "Give it here."

"Oh, no, it's not expired, it's all right, I think I just

inserted it wrong," Ivor snatched the card out of the reader and gave it to Dana. "Here, would you like to put it in for me?" He picked up the device so she could see it more clearly. "See how it works? Put it in the slot with the black stripe up, and then this computer talks to another computer at the bank."

Dana saw the card had expired, and realised that Ivor must want her to make the computer think it hadn't. She put it back into the reader. This time it beeped, and the total and the message *Enter PIN* appeared on its screen.

"I have to enter my secret number now." Ivor keyed in a number. Dana didn't wait to see if the computer would verify it; she intercepted the signal and sent it back. The computer started to print a receipt. Ivor took it and gathered up his purchases, muttering a hurried thanks and goodbye to the pharmacist as he towed Dana back outside.

Dana wondered if what they had just done with the card had been wrong. Where did the money come from if the signal never got to Ivor's account? Did the pharmacy not get their money, or had she just magicked up some money from nowhere? Was this what Jananin had meant when she said Pilgrennon would try to use her abilities?

In the car, Ivor unpacked the medicine and studied the leaflet that came wrapped around the blister packs. "Oh, I know this," he said. "It's a concentration-enhancing drug. They've marketed it under a different name than they were using on the trial." He broke one of the tablets in half and passed one side to Peter. "Try this."

Peter put the tablet in his mouth, and Ivor unscrewed the cap from the water bottle and handed it back to him. After Peter had swallowed it, they waited a few minutes. "Do you think you feel calmer?" Ivor asked.

"Maybe." Peter nodded and went back to reading.

Ivor put the paper bag with the medicine in it into his inside jacket pocket. Dana moved her legs to one side so he could fit the bag containing the other things into the passenger seatwell. "But, Ivor," she said, "if he has one a day and there are only 30 of them, they'll only last him a month."

"Yes." Ivor fiddled with the stalk on the steering wheel opposite the indicator, causing a jet of water to spurt onto the windscreen. "That's the maximum prescription you can get. That's why we have to make more prescriptions and go to some other pharmacists."

After taking four more prescriptions to various pharmacists on the route north up the A857 from Stornoway, Dana was famished. Ivor parked at a supermarket and she and Peter waited in the car while he went in. He came back with a trolley piled high with tins, which looked to be rather hard to steer because of its weight, as he was bent over it gripping the sides grimly. After he'd loaded all the tins into the boot, he stopped off at a chip shop in Barvas, and Dana sat with the hot damp paper bag in her lap while he drove up a hill and parked at a layby set aside as a vantage point.

"Isn't it bad to make pretend prescriptions and pay for medicine with pretend money?" Dana asked.

"Yes," Ivor agreed, "but the medicine makes Peter better, and if we didn't do it, Peter would be running around breaking everything, and that wouldn't be fair on him or us."

Peter did seem to have calmed down a little since Ivor had given him the Conurone. He tried to find out how many chips he could fit in his mouth at one time.

"Save some chips for Alpha." Ivor had found some CDs in the car's glove compartment. He put one into a slot on the dashboard. He bit into a pie in his other hand, dribbling gravy on his chips. Piano noises came from the car. "Ah, Rachmaninov! I wondered where that had gone."

"Alpha won't notice," said Peter with his mouth full. "You could give her turds to eat and she wouldn't be able to tell them from chocolate." He had strewn the chips all over the back seat. "She just puts things in her mouth and chews and swallows. She doesn't taste them."

Ivor sighed. "It would still be nice of us to save her some chips."

When they had finished the chips, Ivor looked at his watch. "We'll go to one more pharmacy, and then we need to head back to catch the tide."

"It's *boring* in here," Peter complained. He threw a chip at Dana.

"Yes, well, we're going home soon." Ivor restarted the engine and turned onto the A858. "Read your fish book."

As the car moved away and began to accelerate, Ivor's eyes twitched up at the mirror. Dana looked over the shoulder of her seat and saw a flash of white and blue and fluorescent-yellow paint through the rear windscreen.

Ivor watched the road fixedly, keeping the car at the same speed. The police car loomed in the rear view mirror. Then came the flash of blue light, and the siren started up.

Ivor glanced behind and muttered something in Gaelic.

-14-

IVOR pulled the Landrover into a dirt track off the side of the road. The police car pulled over behind and a policeman got out. He walked around to the front of the car and looked at it, before coming up to Ivor's door and tapping on the window.

"This your car, sir?"

Ivor opened the door. "Yes."

"Can I see your licence, sir?"

"I'm sorry, I don't have it with me."

The policeman looked at Dana, then at Peter, who was kicking Ivor's seat, and at the chips Peter had thrown all over the car.

"Are these your children, sir?"

"Yes."

"Are you aware that this vehicle isn't displaying a valid tax disc?"

"Must've fallen off." Ivor made a point of looking on the floor and moving his feet.

The policeman reached into his pocket and connected a short white tube to a small device. "If you wouldn't mind taking off your seatbelt and blowing into this, hard, please."

Dana watched Ivor's shoulders tense until the object beeped. She couldn't detect any signal from it. The policeman looked at it for a moment before putting it back in his pocket.

"Name and address please?"

"Greg Baker," said Ivor. "12 North Road—"

"Durham!" Dana interrupted, fearing he would invent some nonexistent address in a nearby town with no North Road.

"—Durham," Ivor finished.

The policeman wrote down the details on a piece of paper and copied down the number plate of the Freelander.

"I'm going to have to ask you to come with me to my car while I make some data checks on your licence and this vehicle. And your children will have to accompany you; I'm not permitted to leave them unsupervised."

Ivor got out and opened the back door. "We're going to sit in the policeman's car for a bit. Dana, bring the bag with the printer in it, from the footwell."

Dana faced away from the wind so her hair blew over her face as she got out. What if the policeman recognised her from the news? Perhaps the news in Coventry wasn't the same as here in Scotland, and nobody here would be interested in her disappearance. She hoped so. The policeman looked at Peter as he climbed out of the car. "You're going to have to take that hat off, lad. Those horns could potentially be used as a weapon."

Peter looked up at Ivor.

"Do as the man says, Peter."

Peter took off his helmet and gave it to the man. When Peter had taken off his helmet before in a rage, Dana hadn't had much time to take stock of what he looked like. He had freckles and curly hair a lot like Ivor's, only Peter's hair was bright ginger-red. He gave off a signal, like Cale and Alpha, but not of indifference, like Alpha, or self-contained contemplation, like Cale. Peter's signal betrayed a restless state of mind and an intense curiosity.

Peter looked at the police car. All the small signals emanating from it ceased, one after the other.

"Oops," said Peter.

"You sit in the middle 'cause you're smaller," the policeman instructed Dana. She clambered into the back of the car to sit beside Ivor and pushed the bag containing medicines to the floor. Peter got in behind her.

"Ivor, Ivor," said Peter. "Dana's different from Alpha. She's awake."

Ivor looked at the boy and widened his eyes.

Dana could sense something digging into her, with the repetition of a finger being poked in her side. It was obscene, as though the privacy of her very thoughts was being encroached upon. She shoved it back out.

"Ow-wwww," Peter whinged, palming his forehead.

"Stop it!" Dana hissed. "Think about something else."

The policeman pressed a button on the passenger side of the car's dashboard. He pressed it again.

"Bloody computer."

Peter leaned forward into the gap between the front seats and burped at the policeman. "You smell."

"Peter, pipe down," said Ivor in a weary sort of voice.

Peter still had a chip in his hand. The ridge along the middle of the car where the gear lever and handbrake were mounted had some controls and a USB port on the back of it facing the rear seats. Peter tried to push the chip into the USB port, mashing it to a pulp with his fingers.

The policeman found a device like an enormous mobile phone and put it to his ear.

"Hello, this is Officer Logan. The computer isn't working."

Dana watched the back of Officer Logan's head. It sounded more like a complaint about the computer not being part of his job description rather than a data check. She couldn't feel any signal. Ivor faced her, mouthing frantic words.

"Black Landrover Freelander juliet-bravo-zero-three-india-sierra-papa."

Dana realised he must be giving information to someone else, and that someone else was entering it into a computer. The data was being sent on the giant mobile phone thing, and she couldn't sense whatever signal it gave out. She couldn't affect the data. If only

Peter hadn't broken the car computer. She looked at the doors on either side of Ivor and Peter. No doubt there were childlocks on them, like in Jananin's car.

"Mmm-hmm," said Officer Logan and, after a few minutes, "Mmm-hmm," again in a different tone.

He put down the giant mobile phone and looked over his shoulder at Ivor. "The registered keeper of that car," he pointed through the windscreen to where Ivor's Freelander was pulled over ahead, "is wanted for questioning and has been on the Missing Persons Register for more than ten years. The car's been neither insured nor taxed since that time. Do you have any documentation to prove your identity?"

"Not with me," Ivor said.

"In that case, sir, I'm afraid you're going to have to come back to the station with me." The policeman plugged the key into the ignition. It made a dull click when he turned it.

Officer Logan turned the key again. He took out the key and looked at it, put it back in, and tried again without result.

He put the keys back in his pocket and picked up the phone thing again.

"It's Officer Logan. Look, there must be some rogue signal around here. First the computer broke, and now the engine won't start. Can you send out some backup?"

Over the noise of the wind blowing over the car came a loud crack and a tremendous noise. A great flash of orange light blazed through the windscreen. The windows on either side of the police car disintegrated into tiny cubes of glass and fell away. Small debris rattled down on the roof, and a large plastic object that looked like part of a car's bumper landed on the bonnet and bounced off. When Dana took her hands away from her ears and looked up through the cracked windscreen, where Ivor's Freelander had stood there remained nothing more than a patch of flaming rubble.

"What happened to it?" she cried. "Peter did you—?"

Ivor frantically pulled the doorhandle to no effect. "We have to get out of here, now!"

Officer Logan opened his door and got out. He stared at what was left of the car and held the communicator to his ear. Dana heard only fragments of what he said. "Control! Control! I need immediate backup now!" He threw open the back door. "Everyone out, and keep down!"

They scrambled down a bank and crouched on the grass where some boulders obscured their position from the road.

"Now, stay here," Officer Logan said. "They're sending Charlie November Five."

Ivor turned on the policeman, his manner desperate. "You have to let us go! You don't understand! She's got blood on her mind! She'll stop at nothing!"

"Sir, please get down. You can't leave because I need to question you, and I still don't know what caused that explosion. There could be danger."

"These are my children! I'll not have them hurt!"

"You are in the very best hands, and you can protect them best by doing exactly as I say."

Ivor was not calming down. The policeman made a move for him and a struggle broke out between them. It ended quickly with Ivor's fist hitting him in the face. Officer Logan fell down and reeled on the grass.

Ivor grabbed Dana with one hand and Peter with the other and ran with them down the bank.

"You're going towards a cliff!" Dana warned him. Behind the noise of the wind, a dull thudding sound had come into hearing.

Ivor stopped when he saw the drop. Officer Logan sprinted after them, blood all down his face and uniform. Ivor let go of Dana and Peter, turned back and collided with him. Both of them fell down, but the policeman was better prepared this time and got Ivor on his front and pinioned his arms behind his back. He knelt on him, swearing, as he fastened handcuffs around his wrists.

He was breathing hard when he stood up, wiping his bloody face on the back of his hand. "Idiot." He pointed to Dana and Peter. "You two stay here, and stay away from the edge!" He turned and ran back up towards the road.

Dana could feel little bits of data streaming from something. The continuous throb intensified.

Control, this is Charlie November Five. We've located Officer Logan's patrol car, over.

Roger, Charlie November Five. Proceed with caution. Over.

Dana turned her face to the sky, trying to see where it was. Charlie November Five was a very silly name to give a helicopter.

"Dana." Ivor twisted so he could see her. "Where's the bag with the printer and the stuff I bought at the pharmacy? It's got tools in it that might be able to cut through this. Please don't tell me it got left in my car?"

"No, I brought it with us." Dana thought back to when she had last seen it. "It's in the police car."

"You're going to have to go and get it. And Peter, you go too and get your helmet back."

Dana and Peter climbed back up the incline to the car. The doors were still open. Farther down the road, Officer Logan was waving his arms about in the wind. The noise was much louder now, and she could see the helicopter in the distance. She dragged the bag across the seat and out of the car. Peter climbed across the driver's seat to get his helmet. As Dana stepped away from the door, she felt the car move. Peter looked out in alarm as it slid backwards.

"The handbrake must be off!" Dana realised "Peter, get out quick!"

Peter stumbled and fell, the car's door passing over him as it gathered speed. The bonnet reared as it went over the edge of the road and down the precipice, showering Peter with mud and gravel. The back left wing hit the ground below with a sound of crunching glass and metal. It tilted backwards and rolled over twice, its door opening and closing like the pectoral fin of a dying fish. The car came to rest on its roof, the underside of it a vulgar steel nudity of machinery and pipes.

Dana clutched the bag and went back to Ivor.

"Find the pliers, quickly!" he told them. "No, Peter, let Dana do it! You keep watch for me instead!"

Dana took the pliers from Peter. She clamped the steel beak around the chain between the handcuffs holding Ivor's arms behind his back and gripped the opposing handles. She pulled with all the strength she could muster. A grating noise and a thunk, and the middle link on the chain broke in two. Ivor pulled his arms free and got to his knees.

Up on the road, Officer Logan was shouting, "It was here a moment ago! It can't just vanish!"

"Ivor, can you drive a helicopter?" Dana asked.

Ivor grimaced. "I had a few lessons. Back in the days when I had more money than sense."

She concentrated on where she had found the voices. Carefully, she moulded the intonations of the voice that called itself Control into the radio signal.

Charlie November Five, this is Control! Officer Logan requests immediate assistance. Please land and go to help him. Over.

The pause between the transmission and the reply seemed to take an age.

Roger, control! Over and out!

"This way!" Dana led the way to the place the helicopter was landing. She saw the undercarriage, with sled-like runners, come down on the road, and the police all jumped out and ran towards Officer Logan. The noise of the slowing rotors was deafening as they approached the helicopter. The wind it generated tore at Dana's hair and pressed her down.

They reached the edge of the road unnoticed. Ivor clambered in and pulled up Dana and Peter.

A man sat at the controls, and he stood upon seeing them and started forward. Ivor met him with a scuffle in which the pilot was turned about and pushed out through the door they'd come in. Ivor slammed the sliding door and went forward to the seats.

"They've seen us!" Dana cried. Through the window, the police were running back up the road, shouting.

Ivor braced his feet against some pedals on the floor. Dana's stomach dipped as the helicopter elevated twenty feet into the air, leaving the policemen below. Immediately, it began to drift right. Ivor pulled a lever and the helicopter pitched left hard. It lurched and hove forward towards the coastline, out and away from the police below. The landscape swung sickeningly past the window. Loch Ròg and its cluttered archipelago sped by.

"Are we going to keep this helicopter?" Peter shouted gleefully.

"No, we're going to park it and leave it and go back to Roareim on our boat that we came on. Maybe if we don't damage it, they won't kick up too much of a stink and come looking for us."

The shattered concrete buildings of Gallan Head swung past the windows, looking like discoloured white Lego bricks scattered on the rock from this height. Dana hung on to Ivor's seat. Aird Uig passed in a flash, then a lot of rock, and then the cove opened out in front of the helicopter, the boat still beached on the sand, waves lapping at its keel. Ivor turned in to land the helicopter on the flattened area beyond the headland.

A flash of orange engulfed the sky behind, and another great explosion sent the helicopter lurching. Ivor banked hard. "Can you block it?" he shouted at her. "You have to block whatever she's using!"

Dana felt numb. "I can't find a signal!"

When she turned back to Ivor he was steadying the

helicopter. He pressed a switch marked *autopilot* and got out of his seat, pulling her over to the door. "Dana," he said hastily. "Whatever happens, keep your legs straight and your feet inside the helicopter and don't panic."

Ivor threw open the door and bunched up a fistful of her jersey and the shirt she was wearing underneath it between her shoulder blades, grabbing the doorframe with his other hand. "Keep your feet on the ledge and lean forward, I've got you, all right?" The thunder of the blades and the scream of the wind deafened her.

Ivor leaned out into the wind, hanging on to Dana thus. Her jersey tightened across her chest as she looked down from the helicopter. The ground was about thirty feet below, and Ivor's grip and the toes of her boots on the edge of the doorframe were all that was keeping her from falling. She wanted to thrash and struggle and get herself back inside. Ahead of the swaying runner of the helicopter, up on the heath, she could see someone, aiming straight at them with a weapon raised to the shoulder, like a gun with a bar mounted across the front.

It was Jananin…

She was lowering the weapon slightly, staring at Dana. The wind flung her brown leather trench coat out behind her and whipped her hair up into gorgon-like strands.

"Keep calm! If she sees there are children on board she might stop! Keep looking for a signal and block it! Break it! Do whatever you need to!"

But Jananin wasn't stopping; she was raising the weapon again, her face set in resolution. The barrel of the explosive gleamed as she took aim.

Ivor pulled both of them back into the helicopter. "The other door! Jump!"

Ivor grabbed hold of Peter, who was reaching over to the console to push a button. He flung open the door on the other side and the floor heaved and all three of them were falling. As the wet sand came up to meet them, the sky was filled with noise and light. At the instant Dana hit the ground, a hot weight struck all over her back.

She turned her head, winded from the fall, to see Charlie November Five crash into the sea as a disintegrating ball of flaming debris.

"Dana... Peter." Ivor's voice. He put his hand on Dana's shoulder and pushed her back down against the beach.

He was trying to stand, but all the breath had been knocked out of him. Dana looked past him, back to the heath where she could still make out Jananin Blake's figure. She was raising the weapon again.

"*Stop!*" Dana sensed the trigger being pulled.

The bar across the end of the weapon shattered into a thousand pieces. Jananin flung it away from her and threw herself down. A long object hurled up, spinning rapidly, then pitched away, pulled down the flank of the coast by the wind, where it detonated with a dull, echoing smack and a flash of light and heat, blowing a crater in the wet sand.

Ivor got up. He took hold of Dana's arm in one hand and Peter's in the other, and he made for the boat where it still waited.

Step by step, they clung to each other, not looking back, and then Ivor was lifting Dana over the side, then Peter. Then the engine was turning over, not starting, Ivor swearing at the boat in Gaelic. The propellers struggled, churning in the silt as he tried to back it out, and although it went on interminably, at last the boat broke free, and they were turning and heading back out to sea.

"Well done, Dana!" Ivor gasped, his attention fixed on the sea ahead as he pushed the boat to its fastest speed.

"I didn't do it!" said Dana. "There weren't any signals there!"

Dana looked back to see a dark figure, now too distant

to make out. The hole in the sand was slowly filling in. She stared at the figure, trying to believe that had not been Jananin up there who had just fired explosives at them. Why had Jananin shot at them? Was it Jananin who had destroyed the Freelander with the same weapon?

"Was it me?" Peter said, his face pale, eyes wide. "Why did it explode like that? Was it because I pressed buttons on it when you told me not to?"

"Peter, no, it wasn't your fault or any of ours."

The Flannan Isles were soon growing larger on the horizon. The black irregularity of Roareim approached, the pylon that supported the beacon and the wind turbine standing stiff in the wind, like dead trees.

Darkness was already forming over the rock in the sea when the boat came about the island and slowed to an idle as it slid back into the cave.

Inside, Ivor went to the kitchen, where Alpha still sat, the hiss of silence playing on the recording he had left for her. "Hello, Alpha," he said, and he pulled her to her feet and hugged her, but she did not acknowledge him, merely turning her head limply so her face was not squashed against his chest.

He released her and rummaged through his jacket pockets. All he found was the packet of pills he'd first bought for Peter. The box was squashed and the cardboard had got wet. He put it down on the chess table.

"All the food, the books..." his voice trailed off.

Dana checked behind her, but Peter had already wandered off.

She chose her words carefully. "That lady tried to kill us."

Ivor glanced at her. He looked away. "Yes."

"Why did she do that?"

Ivor raised his eyebrows. "Dana, I think our priority now is going to have to be sorting out what we are going to do if the police come here when they start searching Lewis to find out how their helicopter got blown up. They will have infra-red cameras to help them, and when they look, there's a risk they could find the door or something else that will give our position away. The only thing that will stop them is you."

"*I* can stop them from coming?"

"No, but when they do come, you can make their scanners show them that there is most definitely nothing on Roareim, apart from a mast and a few rabbits."

-15-

AFTER Peter had gone to bed, expressing concern about the safety of helicopters and asking why people used them if they were so dangerous, Ivor lugged two mattresses into the dining area.

"It's probably best we sleep down here for the next few nights, so we can hear if the alarm goes off."

Ivor talked to Dana as he set about testing the proximity alarm, but she couldn't concentrate on his words. There was a horrible feeling in the pit of her stomach.

Dana got changed while he changed in another room and fetched some blankets and pillows. He let her choose which mattress she wanted to sleep on — she chose the one nearest the door — and wrapped the blanket around her before he turned the light off.

She lay in the dark, staring at the faint blue emergency light on the wall.

"Ivor?"

"Huh?"

"Why did she try to kill us?"

"I'm sorry, Dana, I really am very tired. Can we talk about this tomorrow?"

"Ivor, who is she?"

"Go to sleep. I'll try to explain another time."

Dana lay still, the musty smell of the pillow drowning her nose and the itchy blanket chafing at her neck. *Was that woman the Blake he'd once spoken of,* she wanted to ask. *Why is she trying to kill you? Why did she try to kill me and Peter with you?* But she dared not, and sleep was the last thing on her mind.

Ivor started to wheeze through his nose slightly.

Dana rolled over. She could discern his outline in the dim blue light, lying on his back with one knee bent.

She sat up slowly on the mattress. She detected no change in the regularity of his breathing. "Ivor?" Dana leaned across him and shook his shoulder. He snorted in his throat, the noise masking a faint clink of metal. The key to the main door — in the breast pocket of his dressing gown.

She felt down his front to where the pocket opened. Her fingers closed on the keys. He twitched slightly, as though he dreamed of someone tickling him, but did nothing more.

Silently, she felt about the cold concrete floor for her boots and slid her feet into their fleecy linings. She got up and crept into the dining hall, feeling her way around the table in the weak light, her smallest movements echoing faintly in the cavernous room.

A rectangle of light outlined the closed door to Peter's room. Shadows flitted, as though he was cavorting about in there.

She went through Ivor's bedroom, to the computer room, and unlocked the door. Under the machinery in the crack on the floor, her fingers found the glass vial, safe where she had left it. She studied its powdered white contents in the dim light, her fingers trembling.

Ivor was right; had to be right; couldn't be wrong; it wouldn't make sense if Ivor was wrong. Jananin wasn't her and Cale's mother, she was a mad woman who didn't have autism at all, and *made it up to get attention*, like Miss Robinson had told Pauline Dana did. She probably had paranoid schizophrenia — that was what mad people who thought other people were out to get them were supposed to have, people who set out to kill other people.

She would throw the cyanide away.

She would stay here with Ivor and Peter and Alpha, away from the school, away from the doctors and the hospitals, away from Jananin. And when the police forgot about what had happened, she would help Ivor get medicine to help Peter, and they would all be safe on the island.

Dana locked the door to the computer room behind her as Ivor had told her to. She'd go out through the entrance she'd first entered. That way she could throw the bottle from up high, and it would go farther with no risk of it breaking on the rocks and spilling its poison on Roareim's shore before it reached the water.

She stepped carefully along the corridor to the dining room, watching the flickering light behind Peter's door.

A door opened on the other side of the corridor with an abrupt scrape. Dana flattened herself against the wall as Ivor emerged from the toilet. A blue light was close by opposite him, and she could see he was making a face and pressing his knuckles into the side of his abdomen.

He must have caught sight of her, because he pirouetted ungracefully on his heels and yelled, flinging one hand out towards her while staggering back and putting the other over his heart. "Dana!" He switched the light on, his eyes turning to the key in Dana's hand.

"Dana! You mustn't go outside! It's dark and you could fall!" He put his hand on her shoulder and quickly steered her back into the bedroom. Dana hid the vial in her other hand, holding it in front of her so he wouldn't see it. He took the keys and put them high on the shelf.

"It's dangerous to go out on Roareim alone. You're sensible enough to—" he began. His countenance tightened. "Dana, what's that you've got in your hand?"

"It's just a... a fuse," Dana lied.

Pilgrennon held out his hand. "Can I see, please?"

Dana gave him the vial and sat on the bed without looking at him. She stared at the floor.

"Now, I don't think that would work very well as a fuse."

He was unscrewing the metal cap from the little

bottle. He squinted at its contents through one eye, deep creases forming on his forehead.

"I was going to throw it away!" Dana cried out. "Don't eat it!"

Suddenly, he thrust the bottle under Dana's nose. She pulled away from it, afraid of what he might do. An unpleasant almondy smell pierced her throat and made her cough.

Pilgrennon calmly screwed the lid back on the vial. "It's cyanide, isn't it?" he said. "Some people can smell cyanide, and some people can't. It's genetic, and children can inherit it from their parents. Not many people would know that I can't smell cyanide, and of those, I believe only one would be able to obtain it. And, certainly, only she would entrust it to a child. Dana, you've seen that woman who shot at the helicopter before, haven't you?"

<h1 style="text-align:center">-16-</h1>

“**I WAS** going to throw it away,” Dana repeated, but her voice sounded uncertain.

Ivor did not speak for what seemed a long time. Eventually, he looked at the cyanide vial, cast about the room, and put the glass tube down firmly on the high shelf behind the conkers. He let out a strident exhalation and sat heavily in the armchair.

“I knew from the start you must’ve had some kind of contact with her.”

“What?”

Pilgrennon looked at Dana. “Jananin Blake. When I told you that Dr Blake broke up my research, you said ‘who’s she,’ or, ‘what did she do,’ or something like that. I’m a psychologist. When children hear of Doctor somebody, they always assume that somebody is a man. A child with a mother with the title of doctor might ask whether the doctor is a him or a her, or phrase it something like ‘who’s that.’ You couldn’t have intuitively thought, or guessed, that Blake was a woman.”

Dana stared at him. “If you knew, why didn’t you say something?”

Ivor twisted one eyebrow to a peculiar cant, but he wasn’t smiling. “I figured if Blake had found you before me, she’d said her tuppenceworth on me, and I didn’t want you to have any more reasons to fear me. And, also, I suppose, I wanted you to have a sense of security in this place. That way you’d be more likely to slip your guard again and reveal exactly what Blake has told you and what she’s up to out there.”

Dana folded her arms, screwing the seams of her dressing gown up in her hands. “Either you are lying or

Jananin is lying."

"That Blake's vendetta is because of money was a lie, and a weak one at that. She wouldn't have shot at us for the sake of avarice. No, Blake wants me dead, and at that point in time, your sacrifice must've been justified in her mind."

"She said that you stole things from her!"

Ivor sat with his shoulders hunched in his threadbare dressing gown. He leaned his chin in one hand, covering his mouth, his other hand across his stomach and gripping his elbow, and stared at the wall.

"Say it's not true!" Dana screamed. She didn't want to believe Ivor was a thief. She didn't want to believe Jananin had just tried to kill her. She wanted both of them to be right, and all this to be a result of a misunderstanding. Like — what was it Graeme used to say — the wrong end of a stick. He used to say that a lot when Pauline told Dana to do something and she did it and Pauline said it was wrong.

Ivor dropped his arms and looked at Dana. "I stole her invention," he said quietly.

Dana breathed raggedly. "Aren't you going to make an excuse or something?"

"There's no excuse." Ivor sighed. At length, he continued. "Jananin Blake invented a synapse that can join a brain cell to a microelectronic connection. It's a tiny thing. You need a microscope to see it. What there was before that is primitive in comparison, electrodes and the sort inserted directly into the brain, that might be able to send a binary instruction, or operate an extremely crude artificial limb. This was a gamechanger that would allow a direct neural interface with exquisitely detailed control. I approached her, asked her if she would consider licensing it to me, not for profit, for my research in helping autistic children to communicate better.

"Perhaps something about the nature of my research she saw as immoral; I'm not sure. She had an approach from an entrepreneur from America who wanted to use it to help the visually impaired to see using cameras, offering millions, and she turned him down as well, and a number of other offers from what I remember. I suspected she was just being greedy. She was young and she'd invented something revolutionary, and I seem to recall there was some sort of legal squabble with her employer at the time over it. I could see the difference this kind of technology would make to the children I was trying to help, and so I stole it.

"The thing is, Blake's synapse is made of DNA. It's actually very similar to a benign virus, and it can replicate *in vivo*, so once you've got one, you don't need to worry about getting more. I thought, because I wanted it for a good thing, and I didn't tell anyone and kept it to myself, and I wasn't doing it for money, that if she didn't find out, it couldn't hurt her."

"She said you were using autistic children as tools, to control computers."

Ivor gripped the arms of his chair and looked at her sharply. "No. I would never do that. My motivation was always to help the autistic."

She looked up at him fiercely, her eyes burning. "Is Jananin Blake my mother, or not?"

His stare faltered. His bottom lip quivered, and when he at last spoke, he trembled and the word was almost a whisper. "Yes."

"Why did you lie? *Why?*"

Pilgrennon suddenly broke into a sobbing outburst of words. "I don't know. I don't know if, after all these years, I'd started to believe it myself. If I hadn't done it you wouldn't be alive and we wouldn't be having this conversation now. I had my reasons, but there are no excuses for what I did. Purely and simply it was wrong."

"Then who's my father? Did you steal his gametes as well?"

When he didn't reply, Dana demanded, "Are you my

father, then?"

"It's not that simple."

A pang of hate and disgust wrung Dana's guts. "Did you want to have sex with her? But she didn't like you, did she!"

Ivor rose from his seat and pointed a finger at Dana. "Don't you profess to know me; don't think you can divine my past by what you see here now, or what Jananin Blake thinks of me!" He wrung his hands — Dana realised he was twisting that gold ring again. He held his left hand up to her, fingers splayed. "Do you know what this means?" He pointed to the ring, breathing harshly through flared nostrils. "It's a wedding ring. I used to be married — am still married, although no doubt she's had it annulled *in absentia* by now. But I took an oath, and as far as I'm concerned, I'm still her husband."

Dana struggled to grasp what he was getting at. "You were married? To *Jananin*?"

Ivor let out an unnerved, hysterical-sounding laugh. "No, not to her. To a lady called Adrienne." He pointed to the picture of himself and the choppy-haired woman. "That's her."

Dana studied the untidy clothes. "That doesn't look like a wedding."

"That was taken soon after I first met her, not when we got married. Actually." He reached into a drawer on a table beside his bed. "This was when we got married."

Dana took the picture he handed to her. It was one of those photographs only professionals could take, of Ivor and the woman, Adrienne, who wore a white gown. A pale-flowering, leafless tree filled up the image behind them.

Dana frowned. "Why are you wearing a kilt?"

Ivor took the picture back. "Because I'm half Scottish and it's traditional to wear a kilt when you get married. And, before you ask, yes I did wear something underneath it."

"Did you have to leave her behind when you ran away?"

"No. She left me, a long time before I ran away. And it was my own fault. I was too engrossed in my work to notice that my marriage was falling apart." He closed the drawer and sat back down on the bed. "She wanted to have children. And we could've had children, and it would've been great, but for some reason I never noticed that. It was always *wait a few months while I finish writing this paper*, or, *after I've sorted out this grant proposal*. And in the end, she said I was just going to procrastinate forever, and I was more interested in the autistic children I worked with than I was in my own, and that she wasn't putting her biological clock on snooze for me anymore. And she went off and had a baby with someone else."

Ivor cast his eyes down. "I don't know what they tell kids about relationships today, but usually when people have relationships they start out with someone who 'breaks their heart' when they're a teenager, and then they spend their early adulthood working their way through numerous unsuited suitors, and in the end they meet someone tolerant with a good sense of humour, and make do with that.

"Relationships are supposed to be about compromises; you don't get your first choice. But with Adrienne it was never like that. We met when we were undergraduates, and neither of us'd had a relationship before. And from the start, we knew we were right for each other. We didn't squabble or keep secrets from each other. Love isn't about romance, and it's not about sex. It's like when you go out on a wet weekend and it buckets with rain, and you end up eating cold chips out of newspaper with your fingers, in a broken-down car in a layby, and you don't care because the person you're with makes all the difference."

Ivor sniffed. "After she'd gone, I threw myself into my work on autism even more. I have nobody to blame about Adrienne but myself."

"Why are you so obsessed with autism? Why won't you just leave other people alone?"

He was breathing hard, and he turned to stare at the shelf with the photographs on. "Why I'm obsessed with autism? I used to have a sister. Her name was Lydia." He picked up the picture of the teenage girl.

"She is a lot younger than you," Dana observed.

Ivor glanced over his shoulder. "No, she is older than me. She was *different*. The other children at the school we went to used to call her a freak. She seemed to be adapting, starting to fit in, when she was about your age, but when she became a teenager it all went wrong. She got bullied at school and she regressed." Pilgrennon swallowed. "She had this made-up world. She started trying to live it, almost as if she was denying reality. Society wouldn't accept her, so Lydia turned her back on society. She started ignoring people when they spoke to her. My parents made me stop playing with her, they told me — they made me think — she was insane, and, and *evil*. My mother used to shout at her because she wouldn't behave normally."

He had stopped talking and he paced restlessly, his breathing loud. His eyes made wild movements. Dana sensed the chill grip of the underground room's confinement.

"In those days, autism was little heard of, and rarely diagnosed. She would come home from school and go to her bedroom, and she wouldn't speak to anybody during dinner, and then she would go back to her bedroom. She used to draw diagrams and read books about electronics. She used to have this electronics set, and she played with that, until my mother took it away, along with all her books. And then she just sat in there, alone, and stared at the walls. My mother thought she could make Lydia be normal, that if she couldn't have any of the things she liked she would have to do normal things, and she thought Lydia was defying her by choosing the nothing that was the only alternative to the something she was offered."

Ivor turned his back on Dana again and replaced the photograph. She watched him twisting his hands, the knuckles gone white.

"Then, one Saturday, my parents went shopping with me, and they wouldn't take Lydia because they said she embarrassed them. And when we came home, she had dismantled one of the wall sockets and electrocuted herself."

From what Dana could see of Ivor's face behind his shoulder, his eyes were clenched shut and his head was bent forward.

"She was still breathing. My dad called an ambulance. But she had taken all the painkillers in the house, to stop it from hurting, she said, and the drugs destroyed her liver." He turned around, and Dana saw the tears in his eyes. "It took Lydia three days to die. She didn't want to, in the end. She wanted to live and grow up. But there was nothing anyone could do about it. And my parents took me away from her when she died, and no-one was with her, and Lydia died alone, just because they didn't know what to say to her."

He took his spectacles off. "Can you think, when she was buried, what they wrote for her epitaph?"

Dana watched Ivor's fierce, reddened eyes, but did not say anything.

"*Here lies Lydia Pilgrennon. Dearly loved and missed daughter.* Dearly loved and missed; that is an *insult* to her memory!" In the instant of this outburst, Pilgrennon kicked the coffee table into the far wall, breaking one of its legs off and strewing the books and papers that lay on it. Dana put her hands over her ears and flattened herself against the wall.

"It should've said, here lies Lydia Pilgrennon, martyred pariah who died because of her parents' petty pride, much too good for this conniving world. Because that's what it was! What is a society that lets gangs of thugs attack people just because they are different? What is society if society lets parents shun their own child?

"My parents never spoke of Lydia again. They never went to her grave, never celebrated or mourned the days she was born or died. They threw away all her things.

"Years later, when I was doing my A-levels, I read about autism, and I realised that Lydia had not been a 'freak' or an embarrassment, just a girl with a condition that was not her fault. Lydia could've been a brilliant scientist had she had the chance to grow up; as much a genius as Jananin Blake is. My work in psychology gets looked down upon by the hardcore, by physicists and chemists like her. Lydia could have had so much to live for, and it was taken away from her."

Pilgrennon sat back down hard on the end of the bed with a deep shaking gasp, tears flowing down his face.

He was supposed to be an *adult*. Dana turned her head away, embarrassed to see him like this. Perhaps she ought to go away.

"Well, I still haven't answered your question." He made an elaborate task of wiping his face on the corner of his dressing-gown. "Do you know about genetics, and geneticists?"

"I read about DNA," said Dana. "And Watson and Crick."

"Well, I'm a geneticist. When I was married to Adrienne, I was analysing DNA samples from the children in my research institute, trying to isolate the genes responsible for autism. And every answer I came up with just engendered more questions."

He reached to the shelf and picked up a rock. It had been split down the centre, and bands of mineral colours lined its vitreous inside. "The lines in this rock are called strata, and they're caused by impurities. The impurities run through this rock like autism runs through the human genome. I used to take this rock with me when I gave lectures, to use for that analogy."

Ivor replaced the stone on the shelf. He faced Dana, leaning his arm on the edge of the shelf and hanging his head forward. "Where does autism come from? Tens of individual genes, which, when combined, give rise to such a strange, well-characterised pattern of behaviour."

He straightened up. "There's a theory that it's a relic from mixing of Neanderthal genes, and that certain forms result from physiological incompatibilities. But wherever it comes from, the more I looked at my genetic results, the more all these genes started to look like a jigsaw puzzle; a recipe. And when I looked at my own DNA, I could see autism genes running through it just like the strata in that rock.

"Soon after I'd set up my research institute, I was understandably short of cash. I started letting out a part of the institute that we weren't using to a private IVF clinic — that's doctors helping people who can't have children naturally. They had something called a sperm bank, where they freeze sperm so that men whose sperm doesn't work can use it. 'Course, I had the keys to the whole building. I asked some of my male patients to provide samples, saying they were for research, and added them anonymously. Some of the results came back to me a few years later, through my own clinic. That's where Alpha came from. Her parents couldn't cope, so she ended up a permanent resident. I tested her DNA and it turned out her father was one of the patients I'd been seeing around that time."

"So the people who were trying to have children ended up with autistic children that weren't theirs?"

Ivor shrugged. "They wouldn't have been theirs anyway. They wanted sperm from an anonymous donor, and that's what they got. They got children; I got new patients to study how autistic genes are passed on. Nobody lost out." He let out a hollow laugh. "DNA tests, sperm samples. Nobody asks questions when you're a doctor.

"When Adrienne left me, I went a bit too far. I started using genetic engineering techniques to cut DNA from samples into bits and stick them back together. I spent over a year doing this. I collected all the genes I thought related to autism out of samples from patients at my institute and inserted them into a cell taken from me. I was completing the puzzle. Perhaps in some way in my head I was trying to resurrect Lydia, or apologise to her. Then I met Jade Cooper, who offered her services as a surrogate, and it occurred to me that now I had assembled all the genes, the perfect savant could be born and I would see whether my theories had been correct. I was possessed by the idea; it just didn't occur to me that it was illegal or immoral.

"So I stole an ovum from the IVF clinic and removed the nucleus — the bit with the DNA in it — and replaced it with the nucleus of the cell I had altered from myself. It's a technique called cloning. An ovum — an egg — contains half the DNA a cell from a person does. If you put in a whole amount of DNA and charge it with a little electricity, it thinks it's an embryo and it starts to grow, and if you put it inside a woman it becomes a foetus."

Dana squinted at Ivor for what seemed like a long time. "You *copied* yourself, but with autism?"

"In essence, yes."

"You don't know how horrible it is to have autism! You *wanted* it? You're insane!"

Ivor regarded Dana with a sort of resigned, unflinching calm. "Yes, I am. Or I was. I was a conceited young scientist complacent in my knowledge and besotted with my own success, unable to see past the Dunning-Kruger curve and meddling with things I had no right to. And it didn't work.

"Jade carried him to term, but he was born dead. He never started breathing. Somewhere when I was mucking about with the DNA, I must have copied across two complementary versions of a fatal recessive." Ivor paused. "You won't understand that. What I mean is there was an error in my DNA that would normally be hidden, and I unhid it by accident. I was beside myself. I'd spent nine months anticipating my proof, and it hadn't worked. And there was no way I could ever find the error I'd put in and correct it and make another embryo — that would be like looking for a needle in a haystack.

"There was only one thing I could do. Adult men make sperm, normally, but there's a process you can use to form cells that work like sperm from normal cells, that can be used to fertilise ova in a lab. They use it so that a couple who are both female can have a baby together, or sometimes animal breeders and wildlife conservationists use it to restore genetic diversity, from preserved tissue from individuals that have died. The only way you can get rid of a fatal recessive is to cross it out — breed it with another individual without the error, so it becomes hidden again.

"So I started soliciting women with high-functioning autism for eggs. I figured that way, the half of the autism-containing DNA wouldn't get diluted too much. Most of them didn't ask many questions. They thought I was just studying embryos and then destroying them. But Blake *did* ask questions. After all, an embryo can't exhibit autism."

Ivor sighed. "I was the benevolent doctor who helped disabled children. Blake was the elite scientist in the ivory tower, and these old-school academics all think they're above PR and liaising with the public. It wasn't hard for me to capitalise on that. Dana, I don't even know Jananin Blake. I think I met her three or four times. It was by reputation that I worked out she was autistic. Blake's a genius, one of the most brilliant minds of our time; she's proof of the good people with autism can bring society. She never intended to have children, so future generations would have been deprived of that. Your father was a little boy who never got to live, because of a mistake I made. But he was mostly me, genetically speaking."

The underground room had become oppressive. The ceiling seemed lower, the walls closer. "So I'm not a person, am I? I'm just an experiment, on something you stole! So you can have your results!"

"Dana, I was a fool!" He held out his hands, beseeching. "I never stopped to consider the ramifications of what I was doing. I was so arrogant back then. It never occurred to me I would be causing the things Alpha and Peter have to live with every day, or that one day I'd meet you, that you'd be a person I could have a conversation with, whom I'd have to explain all this to!"

"I wish you hadn't told me! I wish I'd never come here; I wish I'd never met Jananin Blake and that Abigail didn't beat me up in the toilet! I wish my real parents were dead like I thought they were, and then I could just get on with being me, and I wouldn't have to be who you just told me I am!" Her voice had risen to a scream.

"Dana, calm down!"

Dana took one stamping step towards him and thumped him on the arm.

"Now stop that!" He flinched as she swiped at his face, and took hold of her, holding her arms against her sides and pushing her into a seated position on the bed. "You're behaving like Peter, and that won't solve anything." She squirmed against his grip. "Now, look, you may be an experiment, but aren't all children products of their parents' experiments? Wouldn't you rather be an experiment than an accident? I, for one, am glad that you are alive today. And as for whether I am your father or not: in some ways, yes, and in other ways, not quite. If 50% of you is Jananin, then 49% is me, and the other one is all bits and ends from other people."

Dana was sweaty and breathless. A numbness

buzzed in her hands and filled up her ears, and the feel of him holding her and looking at her she could not stand any more.

"I can't do this! I don't want to talk to you! I need to be away from people!"

Dana fought free from him and ran into the computer room. She slammed the door and locked it behind her. In the dark, she slowly slid down to the floor, breathing hard, her back against the wall, listening to the reassuring signal of the wLAN and the Internet, and she thought again of the world of the game, with its solitude and wildlife, and for a moment she wished the game were real and what was real could just be a game; to be able to leave her body, inert and unfeeling, and to dwell somewhere unreal, as Alpha perhaps did. She wished that Ivor and Jananin were no more real than a three-headed dog or a ferryman from an old myth, or characters in a game, and to start afresh as someone else.

-17-

DANA had hoped the virtual desert with its beautifully rendered wildlife would make her feel better, that she could forget for a little while what Pilgrennon had just told her and what was happening in reality, but it didn't, not really. She sat on a boulder and, after looking at the scorpions and the tortoises and the little burrowing owls for a bit, she started to cry.

Eric found her there. "What are you doing?" he said. "I didn't realise you could make your avatar cry. Is there an emote command for it?"

"I'm sorry, Eric. I... I had an argument with my dad." When it came into her head, when she said it, it sounded so normal, like something she'd overhear another child at school say. She'd never known what it was like to have a dad, or to have an argument with him. Saying it out loud made it seem a bit less messed-up and weird. "I'll be all right in a minute."

"Your dad, huh?" said Eric. "I've not been on here the last few days because of my mum. She says I spend too much time playing games. My report from school was bad, and she was angry with me. At least your dad's around."

"I have kind-of been staying with my dad," Dana explained. "But it's not working out so well."

"Do you think you'll go back and live with your mum?"

"Maybe." Dana wiped her eyes and sniffed.

"Do you want to see if we can get to Cerberus this time? My mum's gone out somewhere, and it's Friday, so I can stay on late."

Dana nodded and got up from her boulder. Talking to

Eric had made her feel a bit better. Ridiculously, despite what Ivor had just told her, she had never felt more like she fitted in, like she'd just had a normal conversation with Eric about an argument she had with her dad, and he about his mum, the kind that normal children have with their friends.

Eric said, gently, "Do you think you can do your hacking thing, to take us back to the part I keep dying on, and we can see if we can get it right this time?"

Dana wiped her nose down the length of her forearm and nodded. She took hold of Eric's elbow, then she cut and pasted both of them into the coordinates they had last died at, with the boat under them in the Styx just after they had pushed it through the tunnel.

At first it was very dark, and it took a moment for Dana's eyes to adjust from the bright sunlight of the desert. Slowly, Eric's avatar sitting opposite her in the boat came into focus, outlined against the greenish haze of the atmosphere over the subterranean river. Crags shone wetly on the banks. In the water beneath, a fish surfaced with a snatch of fingers into a clutching fist and sank again. Faint echoing noises and the gurgling of the river were the only sounds.

Eric took up the pole and began to push the boat forward. "It's something to do with timing. Every time you try to go forwards, you get washed back, until you capsize or sink."

Dana looked ahead, to the gateway of the two great rocks, barred with greenish minerals. Malachite, perhaps. There might have been a book about rocks and geology she and Peter and Ivor had got from the bookshop that would have told her. An old hardback book with colour plates in the middle pages, she recalled. It had been in Ivor's car when Jananin blew it up.

"Just hold us steady in the water for a bit."

Dana studied the code that made up the game as Eric poled the boat back and forth against the current.

The parameters that determined the speed of the boat were too complicated to fiddle with without risking its destruction, but there must be something else Dana could alter.

"Go forward! Now!"

As Eric began to work Charon's ferry upstream, the flow of water changed as the river detected their approach. As they passed the marble bollards, the wave had already begun, and a massive wall of rolling dark water loomed over the boat. For a moment, fear consumed all thought, and Dana could only stare at the tsunami and the tiny, insignificant reflection of the boat in its face.

Then she copied and pasted the wave subroutine, but with its vector reversed, and clung to the boat's stem as the water rose into her own wave. The tumult of the opposing wave was higher, but now it was beginning to break, and Dana's wave was still rising. Their passage beyond the marble bollards depended on their wave being higher than the other.

The waves collided in an explosion of roiling spume. The impact sent the boat spinning as though it were no more than a walnut shell, and in that instant, Dana knew they were still going forwards. The waves crashed onto the rocks behind with a hollow, echoing noise, taking the boat down with the swell and back into the Styx. Dana and Eric pressed themselves down into the bottom of the hull and tried to hold the thing steady as cold water splashed into it and the boat yawed and pitched, the currents fighting each other.

Dana looked behind to check Eric was still there. The boat was still turning as it drifted upstream, making it difficult to see the details of the shores they now passed.

Eric dipped the pole into the water again, trying to correct the spin and steady their course. They were passing more steep, stony banks covered with sharp edges, no place to come ashore, but he scanned ahead eagerly, and as they advanced, the land began to level away from the precipitous mountains.

"There it is, look!"

The dark form of a large animal had become visible on the shore. At first it appeared simply as a hole in the greenish mist. Then the bulk of shoulders and hindquarters became apparent, and a raised head, focusing on them.

"We have to go ashore and face it," Eric said. "The first time I came here I kept going, to see if there was another way farther up, seeing if there were other options. But the Styx just flows faster and gets narrower as it branches into its tributaries, and everywhere I went the boat got jammed, or grounded itself, and it's just rocks and no way to climb down. Then harpies started coming, and the farther I went, the more came, until they drove me back or killed me. Whatever the next puzzle is, it's to do with Cerberus."

Eric pushed the boat into the shallows and stepped onto the shore. He held his pole, the tip pointed at Cerberus. The prow of the boat caught the bank and the flow of the Styx began to turn it slowly. Dana crouched low and watched as Eric faced the three-headed dog.

As the hound watched him, Dana saw that it did indeed have three heads, but the other two up until now had apparently been asleep, laid across the dog's forelegs in front of it. The conscious head began growling, and the one on the left awoke and added its voice. Eric raised his pole, preparing to defend himself. The third head awoke. In one motion, the creature sprang from the ground.

It was much bigger than a real dog. Compared to Eric's avatar, it was the size of a carthorse, and when it started barking, it sounded like a whole pack of dogs. One of its mouths got hold of Eric's pole as easily as picking a dandelion, and another took hold and the pair of them snapped it in two. With a thunderous bark, the remaining head lunged, striking Eric full in the chest and sending him flying back. Arms flailing, he staggered over the bank and fell into the Styx. The black waters made no sound as they closed over him.

Dana leaned over the side of the boat, searching the depths for him, but he was gone, and so was the pole and the means of steering and moving the boat. The current gave the imminent threat of swinging the boat about and sending it spinning back into the centre of the river where it would carry her away from Cerberus and back downstream, all the way to the river's exit from the cliff.

Dana moved to the other side of the boat and grabbed some greasy strands of brown weeds growing from the bank above the river's undercut. Using these as a handhold, she reached up and dug her fingers into noisome black earth. The boat began to slide from under her, but already she was pushing away from it and reaching. By the time it had drifted away, only her legs remained overhanging.

When she had wriggled away from the water, she turned her head to see where Cerberus had gone. It had settled back down where it had previously lain. The middle head now slept, and the other two heads regarded her impassively.

Most of the enemies in *Pillage and Burn* had an aggro radius, in that if you kept a certain distance away from them, they wouldn't attack, and would just repeat an idle animation. Now she was here and could see Cerberus, and identify the underlying code that made up its presence in the game, it wasn't at all like the pumas and the little owls and other numerous animals that lived in the desert. She wondered for a moment if it was, in fact, another player, like herself and Eric.

She got up slowly and took a step towards it. Immediately, the two heads began to growl. Dana stepped back and they quietened, and after a few seconds, the left head dropped and began to sleep, leaving only one head alert.

Dana sat down on a rock, carefully, because although

the shore was flat, the rocks were still very black and glassy with sharp edges. She looked at the river where Eric had disappeared. Had he disconnected for the night, or had he logged back in and been returned to the beginning? Should she wait to see if he would come back, or should she go back and fetch him?

She studied Cerberus a little longer, but its code was extremely complicated and she couldn't make much sense of it. She couldn't hack it or predict how it would behave. What to do now?

Now Eric wasn't here to talk to, her despondence began to return. She found herself thinking once more of Ivor back on Roareim, and Jananin, on Lewis. Why was it Ivor had done what he'd done all those years ago? And why had Jananin decided that she had to kill him because of it?

Dana remembered one time in the car with Pauline, when the car had run over a rabbit. Pauline had swerved, but the rabbit, possessed by senseless terror, had leapt into the path of the car. Dana had felt the jerk as the tyre ran over it, and she hadn't *wanted* to look in the wing mirror, but she'd had to, and the rabbit was just a ball of mince and fur unravelling on the asphalt.

She remembered Miss Robinson's classroom, when Abigail had tripped her up and broken a computer, and humiliated her, and Dana had wished Abigail dead in a sudden rush of emotion. But she hadn't wished that so to the extent that she would actually try to kill Abigail, with a knife, or by firing explosives at her. It had been more as though she wished some other force would kill Abigail, and that she would rejoice at it but not actively take part in it. She couldn't understand how someone would hate someone so much as to want to do that, not after years and years, and not when it would have meant killing herself and Peter as well.

If Jananin killed Ivor, Dana would never see him stick out his bottom lip and frown when he concentrated again, or cook lobsters, or shut his eyes and lean back and smile when he listened to Rachmaninov, and he would never push Dana on the swings again, and all his wrongs and rights and words would only persist in Dana's memory, indistinguishable from stuff she'd imagined or dreamt. And the world would go on, because the world was a bigger thing, and Ivor Pilgrennon and a rabbit hit by Pauline's car didn't matter to it.

In this game, players died, but they could respawn to play again. In that way, it was not like real life. The animals in the desert, which hunted each other and sometimes had nests and young ones, were more like that. Although Dana had never really been sure, as she'd seen the burrowing owls feeding chicks once, if their populations were autonomous and defined by births and deaths, or there were just x number of owls set to be in the world at any one time, and the game would spawn more when required.

There were several lines of code that made up a wave, and the subroutine got called up from somewhere when certain parameters were true. There were predetermined constants that defined the gravity and inertia. Consequences had to follow causes. The fish-hands, though, they were different again. She could see a few lying about the bank. In their programming, she could see they would writhe and count sixty ticks before they would lie still — unless wriggling and gravity caused them to fall into water and be reset — and then they would go through many stages of decomposition, changing every so often until reduced to a single pixel, and then deleted from the program. They even carried their own DNA; strings of hexadecimal that determined individual characteristics about them.

But these fish were not dead; their code was dormant. Why were they up on the shore, and not in the Styx? Had Cerberus taken them out?

With a jolt of shock as she looked upon them, she

recognised a large one lying close by as being Ivor's hand. She knew it for his watch, a large-faced chronometer with four smaller clocks set within its face and a leather strap, was still bound above the gills on the wrist, and the hand wore his same gold ring on its finger.

Another fish-hand nearby lay crabbed on its back, as though grasping something. It wasn't especially small and it had short fingernails, but she could tell from the long, deft, fingers that it was a woman's hand. It was Jananin's hand. She recalled her memory of Jananin, in the car, her hands flexing on her steering wheel as she talked, those same sure, clever fingers reaching for the indicator stalk or a button on the dashboard.

Had the program taken these images from her mind, of the hands of people she knew? Had sitting here and thinking about Ivor and Jananin summoned them to her?

Dana reached carefully and slowly so as not to disturb Cerberus, and picked up the two fish-hands. They were not just code and images in the game; something else was attached to them, something she'd first thought was a kind of genetic code, an entry, a record in a database. As she held Ivor's fish-hand, the hand resting on its back in her right hand, the still tail in her left, she found she could read the fields.

Dr Ivor Solomon Pilgrennon
Male

And a date of birth, which when Dana did the subtraction made him 41 years old.

Many of the other fields were unpopulated, such as his address, and a lot of other fields to do with voting or elections or something, which ended in an entry that read *insufficient data to analyse*.

Dana set down Ivor's record and studied the other fish-hand

Professor Jananin Blake
Female

And a date of birth which made her 38 years old.

In the address field was an address in Cambridge, and a number of IP address, the address on the Internet where presumably Jananin Blake's computers that she used could be found. The other data on the record were much more complete than Ivor's, and included complex analyses, perhaps of websites visited. Two of the fields said *Consistent voter: Y* and *Leaning: Independent/ Libertarian*.

Dana put both the fish-hands down to the side where she sat, not sure what to make of the information attached to them. When she looked again at Cerberus, she saw there were some more fish-hands lying about its front paws, as though they were toys it had been playing with and taken to bed with it. One of them was a man's hand, with a wedding ring like Ivor's, but all hairy and looking more like a tarantula than a hand, *like Graeme's hand*, and next to it was a woman's small podgy hand with short fingers and a wedding ring and fingernail paint, and as soon as she recognised it as Pauline's, she saw a child's hand, her brother Cale's, and a hand not a woman's, but not big enough to be a man's... Duncan's.

Cerberus was guarding her foster family's records! But *why*?

Not wanting to try anything with the fish-hand of anyone she cared about lest it have unfortunate consequences in reality, Dana cast about until she found Miss Robinson's, with its scarlet-painted nails all chipped and clashing horribly with its skin in the green light.

Dana stamped on it to make sure it was dead, even though she could see nothing in its code to suggest it might come back to life. When she picked it up, it read, *Miss Anna Frederica Robinson, Female. Consistent voter: Y. Leaning: Labour.*

Waving the thing at the three-headed dog did not seem to have much effect. It growled when she got too close, as before. Dana threw the hand over Cerberus's heads into Erebus. The alert head looked over its back, but did nothing more.

Dana stared at the three-headed dog and at the fish-hands. She knew the data the fish-hands had was likely to be the same as those she'd already looked at, and to not make a great deal of sense to her, but now she had seen them there, she didn't want Cerberus to have them, and to know things about Pauline and Graeme and Duncan and Cale. She should take them out of the game with her, or at least release them back into the river where they were supposed to be.

If Eric died by falling in the water, and the object of this puzzle was to get into Erebus, then the obvious solution would be to throw Cerberus into the Styx. Dana picked up Ivor's fish-hand. She couldn't edit the record, but she could pick at and interfere with the code that caused its manifestation in the game. She unbuckled the watch and removed it. If she changed the parameters that controlled the properties of the leather, she could make it stretch. She didn't get it quite right, and the face of the watch stretched as well, like one of Salvador Dali's, but she supposed it didn't matter.

Holding out the stretched watch in front of her with both hands, she advanced towards Cerberus.

Immediately, all three heads came alert. Claws scrabbled on rock as the dog rose to meet her. She repeated in her head that it couldn't hurt her, not really, as it reached towards her, the breath from its maws hitting her face hot and moist and rank. She threw her arms around its central neck and belted the watch around.

Cerberus tried to pull away, but she held on by the watch strap, too close to be bitten. With one hand, she reached for the fish-hands on the rocks below, trying to get hold of them while keeping the dog at arm's length.

Cerberus barked with all three mouths, sending gobbets of drool flying. Dana pivoted on her heels, desperately trying to keep it moving and away. As they fought, her hand got hold of something, and then the dog threw its weight into her and rolled on top of her. Dana let go, but she was sliding down the bank, and as Cerberus splashed into the water, she followed.

She fell flat on her stomach and the water hit her like a wall. The turbulence Cerberus's thrashing churned up obscured her view. Then she was sinking, and the timer was counting. Above her, Cerberus's legs whirled in a trotting motion, heads above the water as it paddled for the shore. With a surge of annoyance, she wondered how Cerberus could swim but she couldn't?

She had retrieved one of the fish-hands, and she clutched it to her. *Duncan Rose, Male*, and Pauline and Graeme's address, and an IP address.

When she looked down, she saw not a silty nor stony bed, but an enormous glass dome with light streaming through it. She was sinking headfirst now and the clock was down to thirty. She looked back past her feet to the surface and saw a floor. At the centre was a space with a table in the middle, and all around it were chairs. The upholstery on the chairs was coloured differently for each 120-degree section of the circular room. It looked like a pie chart in blue, green, and red. She let go of Duncan's fish-hand, and it came back to life and swam away.

The timer was down to ten seconds now, and as Dana drifted closer to the ceiling she could see through the windows of the dome to what was outside. She saw the Houses of Parliament and Big Ben in one direction, but looking through another window, she saw buildings in a more modern style, white cuboids clustered together, with tall fences topped with barbed wire surrounding them, a bit like the military base on Aird Uig, but dry and white instead of sodden and grey and all grown with moss. The window in the other third showed tall buildings, skyscrapers, covered with lights and high-tech advertisements, all in strange characters she couldn't understand.

The timer ended, and Dana was back on the floor in the computer room in Roareim.

Duncan's fish-hand was back in the game. She'd realised she couldn't bring it back with her when she'd let it go, but she could remember the IP address from the record. She used the wLAN to navigate to the Internet connection of Pauline and Graeme's house, wondering, just wanting to feel for a moment, a connection to Cale and to Pauline and Graeme and Duncan, who didn't know anything about Ivor and Jananin or where she'd gone.

When she located it, she could feel data streaming back and forth from it to a gateway. Someone was up at night, playing a game online. It must be Duncan, for the game was *Pillage and Burn*. Pauline had never let Duncan and Dana play online games, but now it seemed he was allowed to. Dana wondered if Duncan would enjoy the Cerberus game, or if he would think it too slow because there wasn't any fighting. Perhaps she could show it to him if she went back. Suddenly, she missed Duncan, and Cale, and Pauline and Graeme, very much.

-18-

IVOR was sitting on the bed when she came out. His eyes were red, and his face and his entire posture betrayed utter exhaustion.

"I'm so sorry, Dana. I'm a brown Midas. Everything I touch and the lives of everyone I know just turns to shit."

He got up and he hugged Dana, holding her tightly to him. Dana started to cry, violent sobs racking her whole body, saturating the shoulder of his dressing gown, not minding that he was crying too, his shoulders shaking against his embrace, one arm on her back and the other clutching the back of her head.

"I'm sorry," Dana said.

"Dana, you've nothing to be sorry for." Ivor's voice broke when he spoke and he squeezed her harder. "None of anything is your fault."

A distant siren sounded. Ivor froze. "The radar!"

Out into the cold, damp corridor they went, to the door, which he unlocked, pulling her up along the ledge behind him, and out into the howling wind.

Inside the island, inside the Cerberus game, Dana hadn't been able to tell how hard it was raining outside. Roareim was lost in the deluge, water pouring down from the cliffs, making the sea boil and swelling new streams in the gullies. Rain thundered on the rocks a few feet ahead of them, beyond the protection of the jutting rock ledge. Ivor slid on the wet rocks and struggled to keep his balance. He set his feet on a stable piece of ground and lifted Dana up to his shoulder. "Can you find them yet?" he shouted over the noise.

Dana stared up into the falling rain. They were coming around the sides of Roareim, two of them.

"Tell their scanners what to see. They must see only rock under this ledge! Not the beacon, not the door, nor the cave where the boat is!"

A great circle of blinding light edged around the cliff and fled across the stony shore. Raindrops sparkled in the lambent cone. The helicopter's blades sliced the rain into black spirals.

Ivor gave his shoulder a jerk. "Dana, if they see anything but rock under this ledge, they will find us here!"

Dana looked up at the helicopter and said nothing. The beam of light twitched back and forth, a restless eye. Turbulence from the helicopter threw spray into her tear-stained face. Ivor stepped back abruptly as the light passed feet in front of them, its perfect circle broken by the rocky edge of the overhang. All she had to do was nothing, and all this would be over, and she could go back home to Graeme and Pauline and see Cale again, and play *Pillage and Burn* with Duncan. The police would lock Ivor up, and that would be better than what Jananin would do to him if she found him.

And Peter and Alpha would go into care, like she and Cale had. And she would have to go back to the school, and the hospital.

"They see only rock," she said at length. "They go now."

As if to confirm her statement, the helicopters turned their beams and passed each other. The dull thudding of their engines died away in the storm.

The noise of rain receded as Ivor carried her back along the ledge, into the rock behind the door.

He put her down on a floor cushion in the warm kitchen. The alarm had stopped. Ivor looked as though all his strength had been washed away by the rain.

He fetched a dark glass bottle out from the rear recesses of one of the kitchen cupboards, uncorked it with a squeaky thump, and tipped some of its contents into one of the tin mugs. Wearily, he seated himself opposite Dana and cradled the mug, the shaking of his fingers causing the ring on his left hand to rattle against the metal surface. Dana watched him. She didn't know what to say, she didn't know what to *think* any more. She pushed sodden clumps of hair away from her eyes.

"What are you drinking?"

"Mead." He held out the mug to her. "It's too strong for you, not that the matter would be the first concern of the police with me."

Dana stuck her nose into the mug. It smelt spicy, vaguely like cough medicine. She took a sip. "It's disgusting," she said, and handed it back.

Ivor took a long draught and swirled the mug, staring into the bottom in the dim light. "It seems Blake hasn't moved on from the wrong I did her all those years ago. Which is my fault entirely. She's obviously used you to track me to where I've managed to stay hidden, minding my own business, for all these years, and it seems she'll stop at nothing to have her revenge."

He adjusted his spectacles, spattered with water drops. "It's only a matter of time, now, before she finds the islands, figures out this is where I've been lying low. I don't know..." his voice quavered, and he raised his eyes to Dana briefly. "I don't know if I can keep you safe here any more. The decision is for you to make, and I will do my best for you if you want to stay here, but it's in your best interests that she doesn't find you with me. Go back to your foster parents' house, if that's your desire. Find Jananin Blake, if you think she can help you." He paused, before adding, "I don't expect she would hurt you, not under normal circumstances. It's just me she wants. Back there, she saw you as acceptable collateral. I don't know what I will do to protect Peter and Alpha, but at least I'd know you'd be safe."

Dana pulled her boots off. She didn't want to go looking for Jananin, to tell her she had failed to kill

Pilgrennon, especially not after Jananin had shot at the helicopter to kill her. She couldn't imagine Jananin being hospitable if Dana turned up on her doorstep.

She wanted to see Cale again, and Graeme and Pauline, and Duncan. She worried that Cale might have been moved again, without her there, and she might go back to find him gone. She didn't want to go back to the school, and she didn't want to go back to the hospital, where the doctors would find out exactly what the device in her head was for.

Perhaps if she told Graeme what had happened, he would understand. But how would she *say* it to him? Where would she start? A man called Ivor Pilgrennon made her and put a device in her head? A woman called Jananin Blake took her away because she was Dana's real mother, but she didn't know because her eggs had been stolen? It sounded ludicrous, and if she tried to tell it to Graeme she'd mix it up and the words would all fall over each other, like when she tried to explain something she'd been blamed for that was not her fault, and he would think that she was mad, or that someone had done something to her. And he might tell the police and insist on taking her back to hospital to find out why she thought these things.

She couldn't stay here with Ivor, not after he had confirmed everything Jananin had told her was true. She couldn't look at Alpha's empty eyes every morning, knowing that it was Ivor's fault she was born and had ended up that way. She couldn't live like this on Roareim, every day the same, cut off from the world and communicating only with a hyperactive boy with a fish fixation and a man who presented her with aspects of who she was that she couldn't face. She couldn't deal with the truth, and if she was not on Roareim, perhaps the truth would not be there. It would be like a strange, disturbing dream, its unsettling dread quickly forgotten in the hours of dawn. And she could just be Dana Provine who didn't know who her ancestors were or the story of her birth.

Ivor stared at his mug. "Whatever happens, Dana, whatever you decide, I want you to know, to always remember, that you were wanted. And that you are perfect in every way that you are, and that it's an absolute honour I am in no way deserving of to have a daughter like you."

"When?" She didn't look at him.

"I can probably go tomorrow, as long as things have died down a bit, and so long as you're confident you'll be able to get off the beach and find your way from there on your own steam. If you can hang on a bit longer, I can perhaps get you to a port or a train station in Skye."

Dana didn't reply for a long time. All her life, other people had made her decisions for her, whether to stay in a foster situation, whether to be moved on, to be sent to school. Now the choices spread before her were her own to make, but none of them seemed very hopeful.

"Let's go in the morning, then."

-End of Book One-

PILGRENNON'S GAMBIT

MANDA BENSON

-Book two of Pilgrennon's Children-

There's a reason why the same government has been in power for so long. It's the same reason everyone who knows why is either dead or missing.

Dana Provine ran away from home, unable to face another day of school or the doctors who discovered a device implanted in her brain. Jananin Blake turned away from a successful career to seek revenge for an abuse committed against her in the name of science. Ivor Pilgrennon spent years in hiding, facing daily the consequences of his unethical research. When Dana attracts the attention of an AI supercomputer with some dangerous connections and the power to destroy everything she knows, the three of them are forced to work together. Can old enmities be overcome for the greater good, or will the grievances of the past end any hope for a future?

www.tangentrine.com

PILGRENNON'S CHILDREN

THE PENTALOGY

PILGRENNON'S BEACON

PILGRENNON'S GAMBIT

THE EMERALD FORGE

THE LAMBTON WORM

THE FROZEN SHORE

9 781917 231015